BEYOND THE
PHYSICAL

By

Charles E. Gaskin

8/25/03

ISBN: 0-7596-7206-7 (e-book)
ISBN: 0-7596-7207-5 (Paperback)
ISBN: 1-4033-1313-X (Dustjacket)

This book is printed on acid free paper.

1stBooks — rev. 12/09/02

AS THE ANGEL TALKED WE MOVED IN SPIRIT

THAT WHICH I HAVE ALWAYS FEARED AS THE END OF LIFE, I NOW SEE AS THE BEGINNING OF LIFE- A TRANSITION INTO A GREATER LIFE, WHICH HAS NO END. THIS ACCOUNT TELLS OF REAL EVENTS THAT WERE THE BASIS OF A WONDERFUL JOURNEY TO, AND REVELATION OF, A TIME AND PLACE BEYOND OUR PHYSICAL EXISTENCE AND THE PROMISE OF GREATER THINGS TO COME.

This story is one more of the many modern-day spiritual experiences. I believe that the real miracle in this case was that I did not have to die in order to view and understand what's beyond our physical world. Life truly is wonderful and everlasting. Yes, that old saying is true: "We are all just travelers passing through this world."

A true life experience.

DEDICATION

This book is dedicated to the understanding of God's purpose and desire for mankind. It is also dedicated to my loving wife, Glenda and children, Petrice J. and Charles Jr. My family has been a tremendous support and inspiration to me. I also dedicate it to the memory of my mother and father, George and Carrie Gaskin. They provided me with much love, insight and inspiration, even as they struggled to raise eleven children during a difficult time. It was the teachings and words of my mother during my early childhood that has given me a greater awareness of God's presence in my life and the world. My attitude toward life and my fellow man is greatly influenced by the teachings of my mother and father. I also dedicate this book to my brothers and sisters; Dora M. (Gaskin) Hunter, Bertiel (Gaskin) Harris, Elmira Gaskin, Thelma R. (Gaskin) Newsome, Wade D. Gaskin, Jessie L. Gaskin, Dan W. Gaskin, Robert L. Gaskin, Frank J. Gaskin and David L. Gaskin. These are the people that have help shape my life and at all time showed great love and understanding.

AUTHOR'S NOTES

In the search for knowledge, wisdom and understanding, you will find many things along the way. The search for knowledge and wisdom in itself will yield much understanding. Life on earth is a beginning place for a much greater and everlasting life. There are many events that indicate the presence of other spiritual beings in our world. Many books and stories have been dedicated to the exploration and revelation of those encounters. My life has taken on an entirely different meaning and purposes since my own spiritual encounter some twenty years ago.

At one time, twenty years seemed like a long time. Now I better understand time's relationship to life. Time is insignificant, because my life is not bound by time. My real life is eternal and everlasting. Thanks to what I experienced, and what was revealed to me, I can clearly see that which I so often wondered about earlier in my life. Even if any of us should live to be one hundred or more years in age, we would still be infants in the reality of life and time. Compare eighty years of physical life to nine hundred trillion or more years of life, and see how insignificant what we strive to accumulate here on earth is to the total life of a being. Sure we want to enjoy life here on earth, but we must remember it is better to prepare for the eternal portion of that life. In doing so we must always remember our creator, and do the right thing.

CONTENTS

WE ARE TRAVELERS, MOVING FROM YEARS TO ETERNITY. WE ARE TRAVELING THROUGH A REALM WHERE LIFE IS MEASURED IN TIME; OF WHICH WE FEEL WE DO NOT HAVE ENOUGH, TO A REALM WHERE WE HAVE ALL ETERNITY, AND TIME HAS LITTLE EFFECT ON OUR EXISTENCE.

Today, we hear of many people who experience miracles and spiritual encounters. It appears that God has increased His efforts to get our attention. There seem to be more reported sightings and encounters with angels than ever before in our modern age. God is constantly making us aware of His presence and ability to help us in any situation.

One quiet spring night, I had an unusual experience, which changed my entire life, and how I view everything. On this night while I lay in my bed sleeping, an Angel of the Lord appeared and spoke unto me, saying, ***"There are some things that I want to show you."*** My first thought was: "Is this my death?" At the sound of his voice I did not worry and submitted myself to him. At that moment I was in the spirit. As we moved it was as if he were carrying me, not physically, but guiding my spirit as we traveled. We were moving in spirit as I moved beyond the realm of the known. As this was happening to me, I knew that it was real. I asked myself: "Is this really happening to me?" At this moment I had no sense of physical being, and only look forward to what was about to happen.

What happened during this encounter and the events that followed in my life has had a profound effect on every aspect of my life in the physical world. These events are modern day messages to alert us that we are not alone, and that we have great purpose in God's plan.

FOREWORD

We are all spiritual beings. We are spirits first, with a physical body that enables us to experience the physical world in a way suitable to God's plan for us. If we never experience the things that are in this world, then how can we truly appreciate what God has in store for us? Without knowing sickness and pain, how can we appreciate eternal health, wholeness and the complete absence of pain? Without experiencing hate, how can we fully appreciate God's eternal love? Without experiencing ignorance and lack of knowledge how can we appreciate the total knowledge and understanding, which the Lord has in store for us?

Lucifer and his followers never knew these physical and spiritual difficulties, and therefore they did not appreciate all that God had given them. Perhaps if they had experienced these physical and spiritual pains, they would have better appreciated God's love and goodness.

Our life on this earth has great purpose. That purpose is to serve God in all that we do, and learn from the experiences of pain, sorrow, sickness, love, hate, lust, honesty, dishonesty, and so on. When we are joined once again with our maker, perhaps we will be truly appreciative of his gifts to us. We are all connected and part of a much larger picture than many of us know or understand.

The pages that follow examine instances of God's intervention in my life, and reveal some of the things that God wants us all to know about Him and ourselves. The experiences show how God performs small and large miracles, and announces His presence in a profound way, which can not be denied. God's promises are made known in the Bible and other religious texts within our society, along with his revelation to modern day saints and prophets. We can all have a close and personal relationship with God by allowing him to work in our lives, and being able to recognize His presence.

Experiences and insights within this book can serve as a guide and source of encouragement for each of you as you experience and journey through life. Remember all that happens to us has purpose and is intended to aid us in learning. However disappointing some events may be in our lives, they are only temporary and are intended to help us develop as stronger, more knowledgeable and spiritually aware beings. The purpose of this book is to show that God's promises of life beyond our present physical condition, and life eternal, are true. It is also intended to help young people gain a greater understanding of life and death.

C.E.G.

2

FOUNDATION FOR A
SPIRITUAL LIFE AND
EXPERIENCES

Everything has an origin. In fact, any type of growth, be it spiritual, intellectual, or personal, requires a sound foundation. I consider my parents, and our local community to be the foundation for my own spiritual growth. When I say community, I mean neighbors, local schools, and the church. As the old African proverb goes, "It takes a whole tribe to raise a child."

I grew up in a typical Southern Baptist environment, in rural Vicksburg, Mississippi. We went to Sunday school every Sunday and to church regularly. This proved to be the most influential institution of my early years.

In our community neighbors were the same as parents. It was understood by all neighbors that if any child was caught doing something wrong, that it was the neighbor's responsibility and obligation to correct, teach, and even discipline that child. Since most of the neighbors were also members of the community church, it was difficult for a child to get away with anything. The family names within our community will always remind me of my upbringing. Some of the sir names of the families were: Neal, Andrew, Stewart, Winston, Kline, Smith, Washington, Wilson, Hicks, Gardner, Higgins, Gaskin, Bernard, Flowers, Watkins, Whitaker, Brisco, Elmore, Pendleton, Jones, Brown, McGee, and Harris. These were different family groups; but we were all close, like one family.

Unfortunately that does not exist in our society today. Hardly any parent will allow another person to discipline their children or to teach them in the area of morals and Christian belief. As a matter of fact, many parents do not want anyone to correct their child, even if the child is wrong and disrespectful. As an observation of today's young parents, too many of them support their children's wrong doing, even when the child is completely in the wrong.

At school, the teachers taught us how to behave and live. They taught morals, behavior, self-discipline, honor, patriotism, as well as math, grammar, reading, science, and history. Our society and lawmakers have made it very difficult for schools to provide children with all these fundamentals today-fundamentals that provide the foundation for a balanced and healthy life.

Laws that have taken prayer, the pledge of allegiance and reasonable physical discipline out of schools have crippled educators and society. I feel sorry for many of our young people today. If parents do not teach their children these fundamental concepts, many of them will never get them. Frankly speaking, I believe that a lot of parents do not have nor do they make the time to teach their children these fundamentals.

In today's world many young people appear to be living in spiritual poverty. A great number of them lack one thing that we possessed an abundance of; that is hope for a better future. They seem to have very little to look forward to. Many of today's youth view their tomorrow as a less joyful copy of today. Lust and unbalanced desire for physical and material gains, violence, selfishness, lack of self-discipline and the absence of love and empathy for their fellow man distorts their view of life.

Hopefully the fruits of the spirit, which are: love, peace, kindness, and mercy will fill the void in their lives and enable them to overcome the fear, threats, intimidation and put downs that are a part of their everyday existence. It is my sincere hope that many young people receive these gifts and began to enjoy the wonderful thing that God has given us.

My parents and grandparents served as the center-post and foundation for my spiritual life and development. My parents were average people, struggling to survive. My mother, as with many women during this period in history, did not have a lot of formal education. She had completed schooling up to the eight-grade. In spite of her educational level she was a wonderful person; she loved God and people, and knew God and His word. As I grew up, I saw

God work continuously in her life, allowing her to pass His love on to her eleven children.

My father was a high school graduate and proudly served in the United States Marine Corps during World War II. He was a farmer by nature, as were his father and grandfather. They all were strong men with a strong sense of responsibility. My father was a firm man who was the head of his house. He was firm about spiritual matters, such as the children attending Sunday school and church as well as doing what was right and respecting others. This alone had a profound affect on my life and beliefs.

I recall sitting at my mother's feet listening to her read the Bible to me, when I was about three or four years of age. I recall her talking to me about God and Jesus, and remember the comfort that I gained from listening to her. I recall the warmth of the fire, which came from the cast iron wood stove and which warmed the three-room shotgun house on a hill during the Mississippi winters. The cold air would find its way in through the cracks in the floor and walls but there was great warmth in our home.

The wood heater would consume cords and cords of wood in order to keep the house warm. But the condition of the walls, windows and floors would not allow the heat to stay within the walls very long. Looking back I will say that we may not have had physical wealth but we had great wealth in human spirit.

I recall my mother spending time talking to all her children; but mostly I remember the days of my youth when she spent time talking to me. Her voice comforted me on those cold days when there was nothing to do but sit inside and look out the window at the blue jays and robins, pecking chinaberries out of the yard. The smell of sweet potatoes baking on the wood stove as well as corn bread and greens cooking filled the air of the house. Often, I would just stare at the sunlight coming through the cracked window in the room, and watch the dust particles dance up and down. Even in the presence of all of this, when I looked outside the house to see the splendor of God's creation, I could always see Him in the midst of it all. It seemed that life was great, even though there were many things that we did not have.

I enjoyed the time with my mother on the farm, especially spring and summers. I recall the warm spring days, running bare foot through the young grass, and the smell of honeysuckle. The songs of the mocking bird and blue jay would provide comfort and joy to the day.

Life seemed so good and the problems of life were far from my thoughts. All of this I shared with my ten brothers and sisters. They were more than just brothers and sisters; they were my best friends. Together we had the most wonderful experiences of a lifetime.

During my youth I often thought about life and death. I had no clear understanding of what death was about, nor did I understand the purpose of life. I believed that we only existed on earth and that was the total sum of a life. But oh, how little did I know.

My belief concerning death was; that, when you died, you remained in the ground in some state of sleep or rest, conscious of your existence but unable to do anything. I feared death and everything that surrounded it.

One dark period in my youth was when I was about six or seven years of age. A man came to our home with an adult cousin of mine. For some strange and twisted reason he threatened to kill me. He came to our home on several occasions. He would come up to me and say "Boy I am going to come back and kill you."

As you can imagine, this had a terrifying effect on a child, who knew nothing about the world. This event impacted how I viewed and interacted with everything in my small world. He made this threat on two occasions. From that experience I became somewhat withdrawn, and isolated myself when unknown visitors came to our home. I would take a walk into the woods and just look around at the beauty of God's creation, but living with that fear for a year or more was tough on me.

That experience made it even more difficult for me to deal with life and death issues. This is perhaps when I began to ask myself a lot of questions about life and death, as well as what is the purpose of our lives. Even with my shortsightedness about life and death, I always knew that God, or His chosen angel, was watching, guiding and protecting me. As long as I can remember, I have always had a concept of God, and I have always known his presence. I can not remember a time in my life when I was not aware of God's existence and presence about me. It is as if I came directly from Him and never forgot my presence with Him. But then the spirit of life that I have

4

inside of me is part of His total spirit. For He took a part of His living spirit and placed it in a physical body and created me. We all possess the spirit of God in us; it is the spirit of <u>Life</u>.

As a child I often had insights and revelations but I did not possess the knowledge and wisdom by which to understand what was being given or shown to me. Often times I would journey far from our home; one or two miles just to be alone in nature.

When I made my trips into the woods, I would often sit in a tall tree looking over the world around me. When I looked out over the trees and hills, I could see the glory of God, and feel Him speaking to my spirit.

Often time I would meditate deeply and pray to God while I marveled at what He was capable of creating. I rejoiced at seeing His works and feeling the presence of his loving spirit all around me at all times. His presence was strongly felt whenever I was alone.

It was as though I could see his spirit rising up beyond the trees and horizon like a mist rising from the water. I felt that I was connected with God, and standing in his presence. This gave me much comfort and peace of mind.

I recall another events when I was six or seven, years old that remain one of the most memorable times of my life: God spoke to my spirit. My father was the teacher for our Sunday school. He would often bring home and hold on to the collection taken up each Sunday. During the fifties and early sixties this was mostly a large number of pennies and nickels, since people did not have much. On several occasions I sneaked a couple of pennies from a bag where my father kept them. I never took much, just three or five cents. But one day while sneaking pennies from the bag, a voice spoke to me and said, "You may hide what you do from your parents but I am always there and I see all that you do."

I looked around to see whom it was, that was speaking to me. At that moment I realized that it was not a physical person, but the spirit of God speaking to me. From that point on in my life I knew that no matter what I did, God saw it and there was no hiding from Him.

We often feel that we escape being noticed doing certain acts, but we are always under God's watchful spirit, each moment of our earthly lives. We are not alone even when we do not see or feel the presence of others.

I do not believe that I was much different from any other child during my youth. I walked the same path as most young men, but because of God's presence in my life and the care of my parents, I never committed any acts of violence or anything outside the law. There was always something that would not allow me to go down that path.

The spirit of God directed me to speak the truth and show respect and honor for everyone, especially my elders. As with many young people I would sometimes say things that were not true, and one day the spirit of the Lord caused me to feel such discomfort each time I spoke an untruth that, I had to change. From that day forward, I have always strived to speak the truth.

The Mourner's Bench

The last two weeks of August in each year, our local church would conduct revival. This was not an unusual event, but the way that revival was conducted at our church's revival had a different twist to it. In stead of just being able to confess your belief in Christ or acknowledge your desire to join the church, young prospects had to go through a ritual called mourning.

In the church, a bench would be placed in the front part of the sanctuary. Those who wish to become members of the church would sit on this bench. During this mourning process the people seated on this bench had to pray constantly for the entire two-week period, or until they had a significant spiritual experience. This spiritual experience would be a sign that the individual had been born again in the spirit. After this spiritual experience the individual would become a candidate for baptism.

I along with my brother and sisters always attended church and revival with our parents. We really did not have any choice about the matter, since my father was head deacon.

Finally, at the age of seven, the time had come for me to become a mourner and pray for salvation and acceptance by Jesus Christ. I participated in this ritual from age seven to eleven. This was five years of "<u>Being on the Mourner's Bench</u>." This was a very

6

significant event in my life. This was significant because each year I had to pray unceasingly for two continuous weeks during the month of August. This was a time of heart pouring praying and meditation.

Not only did I have to pray, but also there were certain rules that I had to abide by, while in the status of being on the Mourner's Bench. During this period I was not to play outside, but constantly pray. There was no watching television, listening to the radio, or playing games. I had to go into an area by myself, so others would not disturb me, and there I would silently pray to God and Jesus for acceptance and salvation.

I remember those days quite well. Even while we worked in the fields or around the house, I had to follow the rules set forth for mourners. However there was some flexibility in the routine, where you could carry on some conversation with others without being chastised.

Often times I would go away from the house to pray and meditate. I found that going into the woods was the best place to pray. In the woods there was no one to disturb you and I felt closer to God when I was there. On the ground or high up in a tree I enjoyed the solitude of being alone talking to God.

If I did not feel like going into the wood I would find a quite place in my fathers log crib, where he kept dried corn, watermelons, and cantaloupes during the summer. Often time my thoughts would drift and I would get into a little observation session. During these observation session I would watch insect and animals as they experienced the world around them.

During my prayer sessions I often felt the presence of Jesus near me. Sometimes I would go into a meditative-trance, where I would not be conscious of anything around me. During these trances I would see the image of Christ before me.

I remember one day in particular, I was praying so intently that I felt the spirit of the Lord present around me that all I could do was cry. I could hear Him speaking to my spirit, telling me that He loves me and that He hears my prayers.

I have always believed in Jesus and God and knew they were watching over me. The strange thing about the whole situation of being a mourner was, having to search for something out of the ordinary to report to the church in order to officially be called "saved."

Finally, one day I did stand up and tell the church that the spirit of the Lord had shown me something significant. I was glad to have completed that phase.

Those long days of constant prayer brought me closer to God and made me more aware of his presence. This ritual may seem somewhat unnecessary, but it served a great purpose in my early spiritual development.

The Later Years

After completing high school at Warren Central High School, I entered junior college. The college I attended was Utica Junior College, which was approximately thirty miles from my home, and I traveled there by bus each day. The trip took approximately forty minutes each way. While taking this forty-minute ride each day I would read from a small Bible that I carried and meditate as well. It was an ideal time to meditate, because the ride would put me into a relaxed, near-sleep state of being. As I began to increase my reading, I began to feel the power of the Holy Spirit and the presence of the Lord swelling and growing within me. My knowledge increased significantly, as well as my desire for greater understanding of what I was reading.

During this period in my life, I had several visions or dreams in which I had the ability to travel or move by thought, just by having faith in my ability to do so. On one occasion while lying on my bed in a state of meditation, I experienced a most unique sensation.

While in a relaxed state of meditation, my spirit rose above my body, and could see it lying there still and quite. I recall my spirit, gazing down at the body, and wondering why I needed such a place to dwell. I knew that I was the same person that lived in this physical body. I remember going back into the body as if only drifting back into a bed. I knew this was not a dream, because when it occurred I was in a state of meditation and was aware of my own consciousness and presence.

It is experiences like this that convinced me that life beyond the physical world reflects our true nature and what we really are. This physical life we live has a purpose, and when that purpose is fulfilled, we no longer need its shelter. The power of the mind and the human spirit is mostly unknown, undeveloped, and under-utilized.

As spiritual beings we have many powers, but are not aware of how to tap into those powers. Man's mind is so filled with concerns of the world, that his ability to fully utilize his own God-given powers is blocked. Hate, envy, lust, greed, unforgiving, lies, distrust, deceit, and all wrongdoing block our spiritual abilities.

We as humans are too consumed with thoughts of success, material gain, sexual accomplishments, what others think of us, how can we make more money, and revenge against those that have offended us. Thoughts like these block our natural ability to focus and concentrate. Our lives are filled with so much doubt that we automatically doubt our own ability to do those things that are natural for us. We are told too often that we can not do things. It starts as a baby. Most comments directed toward a child are centered on "Don't do that," or "No, you can't do that." Negative thinking has become a primary part of the human condition. This is unfortunate because this is our main downfall and it blocks our faith in our own natural abilities. It is faith and the spoken word that causes things to happen.

3

SHIELDED BY THE SPIRIT

On several occasions as a child I had what could be called, "near death experiences." Fortunately for me, the Lord who guides my steps, or the one appointed to watch over me, was there to shield me. The first such experience was as an infant, and I was diagnosed as having a severe case of red measles. One of most threatening conditions was that I had a temperature of 104 degrees that would not go down for a couple of days. Doctors worked hard to keep me alive. This was in the early fifties and simple things like this were serious situations, especially when you were poor. Thank goodness I had loving parents who sacrificed for their children. The one thing that proved beneficial was that I was placed in a cooling chamber and given oxygen to keep me going. So, you can see, early on in my life God stepped in and brought me safely through my first trial.

The second situation occurred when I was seven or eight. My brothers and I would often create situations and act them out as seen on television. One warm summer evening, my brother and I were playing cowboys. It was determined that I would be the outlaw. Now it was the unfortunate luck of the outlaw that he was sentenced to hanged. As many children do, we believed that this was just playing and no one would die from playing this game. We would see individuals hanged on television and in a couple of days they would appear on television in another show. To a child, that might give a false impression that hanging is not a killing action.

I recall standing on our small red wagon and my brother placed the rope around my neck and tied the other end around the limb of a chinaberry tree. My mother and aunt were in the front yard, about twenty-five feet away, pealing peaches for canning. I guess all the commotion caused my aunt looked up from what she was doing.

When she saw me swinging there she screamed "don't turn him a loose" and rushed over to catch me.

Being afraid of what my aunt was going to do, my brothers turn me lose and ran. I began to swing and spin around. As I spun all I recall was just spinning and the light seen through my eyes getting dimmer. My aunt grabbed me and freed the rope from around my neck.

Needless to say we all got into trouble for that one. Once again, through the watchfulness of my aunt, God stepped in and saved my physical life, giving me another chance to fully experience His gift of life.

The third experience occurred when I was about ten years old. While growing up in the country, we did not have a lot of recreational activities, but we made the best of those we could find. Swimming or playing in small ponds was one of our favorite things to do. I had a close friend named Joseph Brisco who lived in my neighborhood. I would often walk the two-mile stretch to visit his home on Sundays. I enjoyed visiting his home during the summer because he had a large pond near the house where we could swim or play in the water to cool down from the long week in the cotton or cornfields. Many of the other neighbors would also swim there. I really enjoyed the water and during the summer it was the most fun that I would normally experience during the week. At this time I had no real swimming skills and could only stay above the water for about thirty-five seconds before having to put my feet on something solid. One Sunday several of us were in the pond playing around on a homemade log raft, when a serious incident occurred. I had been playing around the shallow edges of the pond and was fine. But most of the other guys seemed to be having the most fun floating out to the deep end and jumping off of the raft. I decided that it was time that I got in on the fun. The next time the raft came to the shallow end, I got on. There were six of us floating on the raft. We were floating along the shallows of the pond, heading for deeper waters. I was merely going along for the ride. My attention drifted for a while and when I refocused, the raft had drifted quite a ways from the shallows.

The raft was much farther away from the shallow end of the pond than I cared for it to be. At this point, the experienced swimmers on the raft started standing up and jumping off the raft. Their standing made the raft unstable and caused it to tilt and stand on its sides. Frighten and afraid that the raft was about to capsize, I too jumped off the raft. Unfortunately I was too far from the shallow end of the pond. After about thirty seconds of frantically fighting to stay afloat, going under a couple of times, and not touching the bottom, I began to panic and cry for help.

At first, no one seemed to hear me. I suspected that the fact that I had a mouth full of water made it difficult to be heard. After my third cry for help, and my third time going under, my friend Joseph swam over to me and told me to put my arms around his neck. Being as frightened as I was, I nearly drowned him too. Finally he made it to the shallow end with me and I was truly happy to have survived that ordeal. When I got to the shore, I thanked Joseph, and I thanked God for once again saving me.

My fourth ordeal occurred when I was twelve. The majority of our summers were spent working in the gardens and fields of the family farm. The majority of the time we walked to the fields and back home for lunch. On this particular day we were coming out of the cotton field where we had been hoeing or chopping grass out of the young cotton. My older brother, David had been using one of the mules that we owned, to cultivate between the rows while the rest of us were chopping grass. At noon, we gathered up the tools and water containers and headed for the house during our lunch break.

On the way home, one of the boys would usually take the mule to the pond and allow it to drink some cool water. This day I had the pleasure of riding the mule. As most young boy do, I wanted to get a little bit of excitement out of this experience, and I decided that I would ride at a full gallop, as I had seen on television. When I separated from the rest of the group, I put my plan into action. As I passed under a pine tree, I broke off a limb. Now it was time to get serious. I was going to use the pine brush like a whip to make the mule run faster. I hit her on the rump a couple of times with the pine limb and the mule began to break into a gallop. It was fun and I was going to get the maximum run out of this ride. I should note that during this time we did not have a saddle to put on the mule, and therefore rode them bare- backed.

As we proceeded at a gallop; the mule's hooves pounding the ground faster and faster, we approached a very steep hill. As we approached the hill our speed increased. I did not let up until we started down the hill. On the downward slope of the hill, I began to feel myself slowly slide forward towards the mule's neck. Before I knew what to do, I was grasping underneath the mule's neck, trying to hold on. I could hear the steady sound of her pounding hooves and all I could think about was, "I really wish I had not done this...I am really going to get hurt, and this is really going to be a bad one, when I fall." Then, I dropped to the ground with the mule's hooves stomping around me. I rolled down the hill surrounded by thundering hooves. Sore and somewhat bruised, I got up, shook myself off, and thanked God that I had not been injured. Fortunately I survived this incident without a cut or broken bone. I went and collected the mule and slowly walked her home.

Once again God stepped in and protected me from the potentially dangerous hooves of the mule. Sometimes we do not understand what dangers we put ourselves into when we do certain things.

On a farm there can be hidden dangers if you are not careful. A fifth brush with death came when I was thirteen. A typical Saturday during the winter months was spent cutting wood to heat our home. On one particular Saturday, it was getting close to dark and we were heading home.

We were traveling with an old Massey-Ferguson tractor that was pulling an old iron frame wagon, full of the cut wood. We sat amongst the wood, wherever we could find space. I ended up riding on the right rear-wheel fender of the tractor.

It was dark by the time we drove through the dirt roads of my grandmother's farm. As I rode along thinking of getting home and eating some of mom's good cooking, we reached the tip of a hill. As we started down the hill, the long iron tongue, which hitched the wagon to the tractor came undone.

The metal tongue quietly started forward, pushing me off of the tractor. I found myself falling between the wheels of the tractor and the wagon itself. It was dark and I had no idea where the wheels of the wagon. I fell to the ground and the wheels of the wagon hit me as I rolled on the ground. When I got up, I did not seem to have a scratch on me, but I did feel a few bruises. I thanked God once again for stepping in and protecting me from danger.

A sixth situation posed real danger, when I was fourteen, but I was able to once again escape potential harm. One warm summer day, I was driving my father's tractor home from one of the fields. I stopped the tractor on a high hill so I could pick some greens for dinner.

When I was ready to leave, I had to use the "roll and clutch release" method to start the old tractor because the starter did not work very well. I had started the tractor this way so many times. After the first couple of attempts, the starter failed to engage, so I decided to use the old hand crank to start the engine. We always carried a hand crank on the tractor. If not used properly, this could be a dangerous device. For example, if you continued to hold the crank when the engine started, you would end up with a broken arm and shoulder. I made several mistakes in this situation: first I did not set the foot brake on the tractor; second, I did not put the transmission in to the neutral gear; and third, I had left the tractor on a steep incline without any wheel blocks. To start the tractor with the hand crank, you must position yourself in front of the equipment. As I made the first turn with the hand crank, the tractor engine started up. I could hear the muffler popping and the engine rattling. As soon as the tractor started, it lunged forward, and to this day, I don't know how I was able to move out of the way of the tractor in time to keep it from rolling over me. The tractor rolled down the hill into a low-bottom garden area. It traveled in somewhat of a circle, for a minute, until I was able to jump onto side steps of the tractor and stop the engine. Talk about being scared and nervous! I was a bit shaken, but once again, as He had told me earlier in my life, He was watching over me.

The seventh incident occurred while I was driving a small sports car on the autobahns in West Germany. During this incident God stepped in and protected me, as nothing else could have saved me. This story is told later on in the coming pages, as it relates to another part of my experiences.

A more recent experience occurred in the fall of 1996. In May 1993, I was working at the University of North Florida, in Jacksonville, Florida, as an Assistant Professor of Military Science. It was here that I met life-long friends, Peter Ludlow, and Tyran Lance.

As with all military personnel, I went to the military hospital at Mayport Naval Base, Florida, to have my annual physical examination. This time everything was fine except one thing: my hearing had changed since the last examination a year prior. This did not surprise or concern me at first. I attributed it to aging and previous assignments around heavy equipment. The following year I went again for an annual physical and this time my hearing test indicated an even greater hearing loss than before. My hearing in the left ear was steadily decreasing. Tests were conducted to determine what was causing the rapid loss.

I was examined several times by several attending physicians, but they did not discover any obvious causes. Finally I was sent to the ENT clinic and after several routine examinations, they saw nothing out of the ordinary and presumed that it may be a temporary problem.

In June 1994 my assignment with the University ROTC program ended. I was reassigned to the Army Reserve Personnel Center (ARPERCEN), in St. Louis, Missouri. By now my hearing was noticeably lower and it was difficult to hear a phone conversation in the left ear. Ever more concerned about my hearing loss, I traveled to Scott Air Force Base in Illinois to see their ENT specialist. After about three visits and undergoing all the audio and hearing tests available, my doctor said, "All your internal ear organs look fine, but there is one more test I need to run. Normally when all organs check out fine, there is the possibility of a tumor growth. I would like to run an MRI to check for any signs of tumors." He requested the MRI scan to check for tumors, and sure enough a tumor growth was discovered.

Finally, after four years, I knew the cause of my hearing loss. When the problem was first diagnosed, I believed that it was due to exposure to weapons fire and heavy equipment operations while serving in the military. I was diagnosed as having an acoustic neuroma. The acoustic neuroma is a tumor growth on the cable-like structure, which contains the nerves for an individual's facial muscles, physical balance, and hearing.

From the time of the initial notification, I prayed to God concerning my condition and from that point I knew that the surgery and everything else would be fine. As I discussed it with friends and family, they were very concerned, but I never worried about any portion of the surgery or condition.

On my next visit to my doctor, the surgery procedures were explained to me in great detail. I wished that I could escape having the surgery, but I knew that it was definitely necessary. Doctors at Scott Air Force Base explained to me that this type of tumor grows slowly, and if not removed would result in death. The decision was not hard to make, knowing what the known outcome if left unattended. To help me better understand what the operation was all about; I was sent to where the operation would actually be performed; Wilford Hall Medical Center at Lackland Air Force Base in San Antonio, Texas. Here I met with Dr. Charles A. Syms, an Air Force Major who would be performing the actual surgery.

I recall listening to the doctor explaining the procedures which would enable them to remove the tumor as well as some of the possible side effects of the surgery. Some of the risks of this surgery were: hearing loss; taste disturbance; dry-mouth; dizziness and balance disturbance; facial paralysis; eye complications; nerve weakness; postoperative headaches, spinal fluid leaks, bleeding and brain swelling; brain complications, and death. In spite of all of this, I had no worries.

There were two ways by which this tumor could be removed. The first procedure would be to cut a section of skull out of the back of my head, lift up on the brain and remove the tumor. The second procedure would involve cutting behind the ear and pulling the ear back and remove a small section of the skull and go in through the ear area. The section where the skull bone is removed would be filled in with body fat from the stomach. Neither of the procedures discussed made me feel at ease because each procedure required accessing my brain. But in spite of the difficult approaches, I elected the second procedure because it seemed safest.

Between the time of the diagnosis and the surgery I had moved from St. Louis to Clinton, Mississippi, just outside of Jackson, Mississippi. After finishing all the pre-operation briefings, I returned home to Clinton, where I awaited the day of surgery. Three days prior to my surgery I made my way back to Lackland Air Force Base and underwent pre-operation procedures and tests. On August 6,

1996, I underwent this serious operation, requiring six hours on the operating table.

The operation was a complete success. As a matter of fact, as soon as I came around in the recovery room, Dr. Syms and my wife Glenda came into the room. The doctor went through the usual test, asking if I knew what year it was, what is my name, how many fingers was he holding up and those kinds of functional test. Then Dr. Syms asked me, did I recognize the lady standing next to him. My response was "Is that my girlfriend Barbara?" There was complete silence and Dr. Syms looked at my wife with a little bit of concern, and I began to laugh. I figured that I might as well have a little fun, since I made it through safely.

I came through the surgery fine and except for some dizziness and temporary balance loss, I suffered no major complications. I did lose hearing in the left ear, but that was a small price to pay for life. According to the doctor, this was one of the most successful surgery operations for this procedure that he had performed up to that point. I spent one and a half years in recovery. My recovery continues to go well and I give God praise for this success. Today, I enjoy life with just a few adjustments. Life is still good. In fact, life is truly wonderful, with greater things yet to come.

4

MIRACLES

Truly the first miracle that I ever experienced was the day that God put His spirit into me and I became a living soul. Our lives are the greatest testament of God's miraculous powers. As we go on in our lives we see small miracles but will sometimes take them for granted and do not recognize them as miracles. Then there are times when we really do experience or see the really big ones; the obvious ones.

To demonstrate the first obvious miracle, I will go back to when I graduated from junior college in 1974. After graduation, I was hired as a cartographic technician with the U.S. Army Corps of Engineers. This was my first real job, though prior to getting this job, I had joined the Army Reserve, and had yet to fulfill my commitment for training and education.

In the scorching July heat, I attended Basic Combat Training at Fort Leonard Wood, Missouri, and was away from home for the first time. This was an enlightening and emotionally growing experience for me. In fact it was the first significant emotional event of my adult life. I became very much aware of many things during this summer; mostly I became aware of who I was and what I was about, as well as my strengths, and weaknesses. After completing the basic training requirement, I was one happy soldier and was looking forward to my military education in my specialty area.

Basic Combat Training, Aug 1974 Fort Leonard Wood, MO, B-1-3
(*Sitting outside of barracks building with friend Brian Foley*)

After basic training, I traveled to Fort Dix, New Jersey to receive on-the-job training. Upon my arrival, I was informed that I could not start my training, because the classes had already began and that I was too far behind to catch up. Shortly thereafter, I traveled to Fort Lewis, Washington. This is where I experienced my first miracle.

As all new soldiers did, I lived in the barracks, each consisting of two men rooms. Each room door had a latch and lock, and each roommate had a copy of the key. My roommate was one of those guys always on the go, and I very seldom saw him. One Friday evening after my roommate had departed I was leaving the room to go out for the evening. When I stepped out the door, I pulled it shut and placed the lock into the latch. Without thinking any further, I locked the door behind me and started down the hall. About halfway down the hall I hit my pockets and remembered that I had left my wallet and keys in the room.

For approximately one week prior to this event I had been studying and focusing on *Matthew 17:20* in my Bible.

"And Jesus said unto them, Because of your unbelief: for verily I say unto you, "*If ye have faith*" as a grain of mustard seed, ye shall say unto this mountain, Remove hence to yonder place; and it shall remove; and nothing shall be impossible unto you."

Matthew 17:20

This verse concerned the power of faith and what faith can do for an individual. When I first read this verse it stayed in my head and for an entire week I continuously recited the verse in my mind and thought through its meaning fully. I focused on making it a part of my spiritual attitude.

At this point it was obvious that I was not going to be able to find my roommate and that the only alternative was to go to the supply room and request the "universal key," which was actually a heavy-duty bolt cutter. I turned and headed for the supply room. I stopped and thought of the verse that had been in my thoughts over the past week, and said to myself that if faith can accomplish large acts, surely it will work on small things too. I grabbed the lock in my hand and said in my spirit "I command this lock to open in the name of Jesus." The entire time I believed that the lock was going to open. And just as I had believed, with hardly any force at all the lock fell open in my hands. The miracle occurred because of sincere trust in asking God to do something and knowing in my heart and mind without a doubt that it would be done. Miracles are based on faith and trust.

Later that week I was telling a friend of mine about the event. He then invited me to stay with him off base for the weekend. This was a great idea, because I was basically confined to the base without a car, and limited to where the post shuttled traveled. I agreed and off we went. When I arrived, I was surprised to find that several others lived in the house also.

This was the early seventies, not very long after the many social movements of the sixties. The group appeared to consist of individuals who wanted to shake off the cares and concerns of the world, and get back to the simple life.

The members constantly hugged each other and stated their love for each other through out the day. The first thought that came to my mind was that this was a little bit strange for me. It was good, but not what I was expecting. Several of the occupants had sold and given away all that they had owned and were trying to live a life free of physical possessions. The house was modestly furnished with very basic necessities. Though I was unaccustomed to that behavior I stayed for a couple of days and departed. I gained some insight and understanding from the whole situation, and I considered it to be an aid in my total learning and spiritual awareness.

In November 1974 I completed my training at Fort Lewis. Many of the friends that I made there tried to convince me to stay on active duty. However deep inside I knew that there were other things for me to do. I returned home and resumed work with the Corps of Engineers.

After two and a half years I became bored, unmotivated, tired of what I was doing, and I hated going to work each day. Over the previous two years a friend of mine, Mr. Harold Whatley constantly urged me to return to school and do something more with my life. He made me understand that I could be responsible over others and not just subordinate for the rest of my life, I now see that God placed him in my life to provide direction and guidance when I needed it most.

A TIME TO ACT

In the fall of 1976, I cashed in all my saving bonds and returned to college at Mississippi State University. It was clear to me that this is what God wanted for my life. It is here that I became involved with Campus Crusade for Christ; a college-based religious organization that helps young people take a stand for their beliefs and speak to others concerning the good news of Christ and God. It is during, this period of life that I experienced that most joyous event in my life. The following chapters are devoted to telling the events that came about and how they relate to my journey with an angel, spiritual awareness, revelations, life, love, and God's word.

5

VISIONS
BEYOND THE PHYSICAL

REVELATIONS OF GOD'S EXISTENCE:

The spirit of God is always with us, and even more so when we are filled with the Holy Spirit, or Holy Ghost. He is connected with us as spiritual beings. He is the supreme spiritual being and we are created in His image. We are spiritual beings that have a mind (intellect), a soul and temporarily live in a physical body designed for life on earth. God reveals things to us in many ways through out our lives. Sometimes He will reveal things to us through other people, and at other times He will reveal things to us through divine inspiration. Often times He reveals his word and message to us through VISIONS, or Angels, his Holy Messengers.

This fact was made very clear to me at the time I was considering my retirement from the military. God revealed some things to me in a dream that would soon become a reality.

In October of 1995 I had a very unusual dream that provided guidance to me and manifested into reality. At the time of the vision I was working for the Army Reserve Personnel Center in St. Louis, Missouri, and struggling with the idea of early retirement. The dream did not seem that significant at that particular time.

In October 1995 I was nearing a critical point in my military career. I had to make some decisions. I had to make the choice of whether to continue on in the military or consider the early retirement option that was being offered. In an effort to draw the military down to a smaller force, early retirement was made available to officers with more than sixteen years of active service. Many others were wrestling with that same decision.

In my dream, I returned to my hometown of Vicksburg, Mississippi, for a holiday. I was talking to a friend of mine, Earnest Paul Brown, who I hand known most of my life and was also an officer in the Army. Paul and I were talking about our military careers, and he told me that he had retired from the Army and was teaching Junior Reserve Officer Training Corps (JROTC) classes at an area high school.

When I awake I began to ponder on what took place in the dream. It seemed so real that I decided to call Paul and see what was really happening with him. It had been a long time, perhaps about eight years since I had talked with him.

I contacted our mutual military branch assignment officer, and to my surprise, was told, "Paul is at Fort Gordon, Georgia, and by the way he is getting ready to retire." How amazing this revelation was.

I tried to reach Paul the same day. I was told that he was away for a few days, so I left my name and number for him to return my call. A couple of days passed and I called again; this time he was in. We started talking and I informed him that I had dreamed about him being retired. He confirmed the fact that he was retiring and also informed me that he had secured a job in Houston, Texas teaching JROTC. Talk about amazing, it was hard to believe those facts were revealed in my dream.

That vision and conversation led me to the decision I needed to make. After that I was convinced that the early retirement decision was the right thing for me. Along with that decision came some other unique situations in my life, which will be revealed later.

If we ask, God will show us the way and give unto us the answer to our questions- this He has promised. God places people and situations in our paths to show us or teach us the things that he wants us to know or the things that we ask of him. I truly believe that we are existing in the age of enlightenment.

We often view the meeting of someone who gives us some special insight as a chance happening; but this is not chance, for God directs the path of the righteous. He says:

23

"Call to me, and I will answer you, and show you great and mighty things, which you do not know."

Jeremiah 33:3

And Jesus said *"I have yet many things to say unto you, but you can not bear them now. Howbeit when he, the Spirit of truth, is come he will guide you into all truth: for he shall not speak of himself; but whatsoever he shall hear, that shall he speak: and he will shew you things to come"*

John 16:12-13

I believe in these words. I have experienced that, which Jesus spoke of, for I have been shown certain things that I know are things directed by God. What was shown to me, will come to pass, and is a place that already exists in God's realm. The things told and shown to me are of divine origin, inspiration and part of a divine plan. This vision is just one example of the benefits of a close and personal relationship with my savior, Jesus Christ, and our Heavenly Father.

Many individuals view God the Father as some far-removed mystical being, not directly connected to us, but ruling over us. This is not the way it is. He is our real father, just as we consider the human male, whose sperm started our physical life to be our biological father. God is interactive. He communicates to us and protects us. We are merely spirits with a physical shell.

The physical body is only needed to house the spirit, which is the real treasure of human life. It is a part of the father's own spiritual being. We are new creatures. But when we see ourselves as part of God's spirit, we too can say that we have always existed. We are a part of that divine Alpha-Omega spirit that has always been, and will forever be.

Because of this fact my heart is filled with joy daily as I walk about with a smile. I smile because I know how great life is, and how wonderful it will be, once I pass through this life and beyond the physical.

I view most situations in my life as opportunities to experience, and understand conditions, which I will not ever experience when I am with God, or where Jesus is. I am happy, because I know that these things are temporary. I truly enjoy life, and I love all God's people. I especially enjoy people who have a spiritual awareness. One of the things that I often tell individuals who are having a difficult time is that nothing of this earth lasts forever. The only things that last forever are truth, love and God's word.

Today we hear of many people who have experienced miracles and other spiritual phenomena. It appears that God has stepped up His efforts to get our attention. There seem to be more reported sightings and encounters with angels than ever before in our modern age. God is constantly making us aware of his presence and ability to help us in any situation.

People are quick to look for other explanations for miraculous events. Individuals do not want to appear to be too religious. But being religious is not what we want for ourselves; we want to be spirit-filled and led by the Holy Spirit. Anyone can be religious about anything, but being spirit filled and led by the spirit of God, takes on a whole new meaning and dimension of human existence. When I say spirit-filled I am referring to the spirit of God; the Holy Spirit. This has to be clarified, because there are so many spirits out in the world. There are the spirits of lust, greed, unforgiving, selfishness, hate, envy and many others. An individual can be filled with spirits of an evil nature as well as good.

5-A

THE VISION AND THE EXPERIENCE

The following chapters describe my personal experience with God's power and intervention in my life. This event is such a significant part of my life experience here on earth. Because of this experience I am assured that I am more than just a lone traveler. I have the comfort of knowing that there is someone in Gods presence that has been appointed to guide me.

It was spring, 1979. I was twenty-four years of age, fairly mature, and in my third year of college at Mississippi State University. I was becoming more spiritually aware and connected. Long hours of study, and very little free time made my spiritual well being even more important to my health and peace of mind. I was discovering religious organizations and groups on campus. Participation in these groups was helping me develop a greater spiritual awareness.

One of these organizations, Campus Crusade for Christ, made a big difference in my life and encouraged me to be more devoted to the study of the word. It allowed me to become more aware of my own spirituality and to have a better understanding of God's desire for us. As I was coming into this awareness I also would periodically walk around campus and witness to other students about the power and gifts of Jesus Christ.

Studying Gods word and understanding how to witness for God became important to me. My spiritual experiences help broaden my spiritual awareness and stimulated my desire for greater knowledge, wisdom and understanding, for which I constantly prayed. These three elements were really important to me and despite silly and stupid childhood mistakes, I knew that if I possessed these three attributes that I would make it in life. I was becoming increasingly

26

hungry for more understanding of our purpose on earth and what was beyond our physical existence.

As awareness of my own spirituality increased, I knew for the first time that I was not limited to my physical state of being. I knew that, who I was went far beyond what everyone could see in the physical sense. This awareness made me conscious of certain powers that spirits have, and the responsibilities that we as spiritual beings have toward each other. During this stage of spiritual growth and involvement with Campus Crusade for Christ, my spiritual encounters increased. Life was beginning to be more than just living, struggling and surviving.

One quiet spring night, I had an unusual experience, which has changed my entire life, and how I view everything. On this night I completed all my schoolwork and went off to bed. While I lay there sleeping, an Angel of the Lord appeared unto me and said, *"There are some things that I want to show you."*

My first thought was "Is this my death?" At the sound of his voice I did not worry, but submitted myself to him. I was not afraid for I knew what he was. At that moment I was in the spirit and moving in the spirit. As we moved it was as if he was carrying me, not physically, but guiding my spirit as we traveled.

We were moving in spirit, as I moved beyond the realm of known physical limitations. As this was occurring, in all my understanding I knew that this was real. But yet I asked myself: "Is this really happening to me?" At that moment I had no sense of physical being, and only looked forward to what was about to happen next. I was both astounded and delighted at the same time. This is what I had been praying for. I know that people often dream of being somewhere unusual or strange. But this was no dream, as would be confirmed later on.

Looking back on my younger years I recall several dreams or visions where I had the ability to travel from one place to another just by thinking so. In all of those situations I woke up feeling that I still had the power to move in the same manner. The only thing that would be missing was the faith and confidence that I had in the dream.

But on this night it was very real. I was not doing anything physically, and I did not have to concentrate on moving in order to move. I moved at the will of the angel, who was with me. I was subject to what he wanted of me.

5-B

═══════════════════════

A QUIET PLACE

═══════════════════════

I willingly submitted myself to him and did all he asked of me. On our journey I remember traveling to three distinct areas. The first area was a place where we sat and talked. I first recall us standing in an area that appeared to be very rocky, such as a mountain. There was nothing or anyone present except for us; everything else appeared dark and quiet. It was a place of solitude, a place where he knew we would not be disturbed.

In the vision the angel took me to a place that was dark and rocky, where he talked to me about how I should live as a spiritual being.

As the angel spoke I listened. I was eager to learn, and listened with great anticipation as he spoke and instructed me. I was so consumed by the glory of the moment that I was not completely aware of all that was happening to me. My first thought was: this is so unbelievable, for I knew that it was more than just a dream. Never before, had I even had a dream of such magnitude or power. This was my first encounter with a real angel in any form. As I write I do not recall all of the conversation between us. I recall that he was instructing me concerning the way that I should live and how to deal with others- for what we do for others is one of the few things that are of any real importance in our lives.

Serving self has no rewards or affect on spiritual growth. We are here to love and help one another to gain the experiences that life on earth has to offer. From what I recall, most of his conversation was about love, understanding, patience, forgiving, and the nature of man. And in the area of love and understanding it should be made clear that all people are the same. Neither color, nationality nor religious denominations mean any thing in the true sense of human existence. In his presence I understood that the greatest gifts of all are to love and show patience and understanding. Love is the great power that defines, moves and penetrates everything. When we love we are living out the true purpose for our existence; through love, the true nature of God's creation is shown. <u>When we love we are experiencing and exercising the power of God.</u>

My spirit was delighted and felt honored that I had been chosen to experience all of this. Even though I can not recall all that was said during our time together, I am sure it is still in the sub-conscious realm of my mind.

As spiritual beings we have much more ability than we realize. We do not realize it because we are so caught up with the insignificant things of the world. We do not think that they are insignificant but they really do not transcend or add to anything beyond the physical life. That is the true measure of value. <u>If it can transcend beyond the physical, then it has real value.</u>

Now that he had made me aware of all that I needed to know, he spoke and said, "*I have more to show you.*" Once again, in the spirit we began to travel. He was now ready to show me the things that were required for me to see. Once again I felt overjoyed and completely at peace and at home with the holy messenger. When in his presence I felt safe and secure. I also had the feeling that he was someone that I knew and served a special purpose in my life; not just my physical life but also my spiritual life beyond the physical world.

The Joy and Peace of Spiritual Freedom

It is amazing how much of a burden our everyday concerns about job, finance, education, and success place on our peace of mind and spiritual wellness. During my journey with the angel, I was completely free of the worries and cares of the world I had left behind. It is difficult to express the peace one experiences in the spiritual state; unburdened by the limits and cares of the flesh. The joy is indescribable; it penetrates every fiber of you being. No experience in my physical life has left me with such an everlasting sense of joy, peace and being alive. This is more than just a feeling-it is the reality of life.

By now I was fully aware of what was happening to me, and I had no doubt that the one with me was acting on the will of Jesus or GOD the Father. What an amazing experience; here I am walking and talking with one sent by God. I felt truly blessed, that God would send a message to me. This is a moment that I will cherish for life.

This was as real as any other life experience. It was all so evident; I was not dreaming. There was just something about the things around me that told me that this is the real world outside of our physical prison. Later on I would have more experiences that would reaffirm the reality of it all.

God understands the mind of man, and He knew that there had to be some experience past the vision to show the reality of what He had shown. Those experiences were soon to come in my life.

Some years after this experience, I find great comfort in the following words found in the book of Revelation, written by John concerning the things that happened to him when he was given the revelation of the second coming of Christ.

"After this I looked, and behold, a door was opened in heaven: and the first voice which I heard was as it were of a trumpet talking with me; which said; come up hither, and I will shew thee things

31

which must be hereafter". (2) And immediately I was in the spirit: behold, a throne was set in heaven and one sat on the throne".

Revelation 4: 1-2

"And he said unto me, these sayings are faithful and true: and the Lord God of the Holy prophets sent his angel to shew unto his servant the things, which must shortly be done."

Revelation 22:6

I realized that there was purpose for all that was happening, but it had not yet come clear to me as to why I had been chosen to see these things. Yet, I was more than delighted that it was happening. Few people have spoke of having such an experience in their earthly lifetime. The desire to know what is beyond the physical has always been man's greatest quest. Here I am standing beyond where most living beings have ever been, and all I wanted was to see and know is more!

5-C

===

THE WATERS OF LIFE

===

Time was no longer important, and in fact time had no meaning at all. My spirit felt as light as a summer breeze and I no longer felt the presence of my physical body. It did not seem as if we had traveled long when we came to the second location. This place was, quiet and peaceful- more peaceful than any place that I have ever known in my life. What was happening to me was so remarkable that it could not be explained by what I knew in my physical world.

The sights that surrounded me were like a world that was clean and untouched. What I was seeing was like a summer meadow filled with all types of beautiful wild flowers and plants. There was also a cool clear running stream running through the flowers, and mountains in the far distance.

This was a special place and it filled all my senses with joy. I truly felt at home and that this was where I belonged. We talked and casually walked among flowers and plants in this lush and beautiful place. Through this meadow ran a quiet, soothing stream, flowing through the flowers and then out of sight. The rhythm of its movement soothed and relaxed me as I watched it flow. I could hear every sound. But still there was peace and quiet.

We continued to talk as he walked ahead of me, leading me toward the mountains. I was so much at peace that I just wanted to continue in the presence of this being. I looked forward to each word that he had to say. Now about this time I am beginning to feel further and further removed form the physical world; so far that I do not anticipate returning. I am feeling so happy and satisfied that returning to the physical world is not a concern of mine. Once beyond the physical, life takes on a whole new dimension; one that is indescribable and exhilarating.

I am not sure of the symbolic representation of the stream, unless it represented life in its desired state: pure, relaxing, enjoyable, untroubled and flowing freely. The running waters of the stream could have been a reference to the nature of Jesus, who represents the living waters that flow from the new city.

This living water possesses the love of God, which represents the son, Jesus. This may explain why the feeling of calm, love and peace penetrated everything I saw and touched, as we walked in the valley towards the mountains. At that moment I did not yet realize just how special this place was.

In Revelations, John spoke of a river of water that he saw in the new city.

"And he shewed me a pure river of water of life. Clear as crystal proceeding out of the throne of God and of the Lamb."
Revelation 22:1

I was completely relaxed and at peace. As we walked in the beautiful tall grass I remembered a personal fear of snakes, and I began to hesitate on taking my next steps. I occasionally look down as I walked, but he that was with me, knew my fears, and me and said to me, *"Do not be afraid for there are no snakes here."* After hearing this, I no longer felt hesitation or anxiety and really began to enjoy the beauty and wonder of this marvelous place. It was earth at its best: no noise, no pollution, no planes, nothing but God's best and most beautiful creations. This is what I would call "New Earth."

This place gave me a sense of peace that would remain with me the entire time that I was with the angel; a peace such as I have never experienced in my entire physical life. *Oh, how I long for that peace again*. The warmth and beauty of this place filled me with much joy. The air and every particle around me seemed to echo love and joy. It was the feeling of love, peace, and joy that seemed to resonate in the air, and in every particle. These are the things I remember most whenever I recall these experiences. The love of the one with me, as well as God's love filled this place. This love penetrated me as well as everything around it. It was the clearest, quietest day I have ever known. So beautiful, bright, and cheerful was this place, yet I don not recall seeing a sun. In revelations, I also found a reference to this part of the experience:

"And the city had no need of the sun, neither of the moon, to shine in it: for the glory of God did lighten it, and the Lamb is the light thereof".

Revelation 21:23

5-D

BEYOND THE MOUNTAINS
LIES THE NEW CITY

The Angel proceeded ahead of me and continued to speak as we moved. Our movement and conversation existed in a spiritual realm. He knew my thoughts and I knew his thoughts. As we walked, he spoke to me concerning the spirit of forgiveness. He stated that without a forgiving spirit, we could destroy ourselves with the evil that exists in an unforgiving spirit.

As we came near the mountain we stopped and he spoke, saying: *"Beyond the mountain lies the New City but you will not see it now."* Even though in my heart I desired to see the new city, I was content just knowing that it was there, beyond the mountains where we stood. I did not see the city, but I knew in my spirit that it was present and that it represented eternal life, as well as Jesus' promise to us:

"And if I go and prepare a place for you I will come again and receive you to myself; that where I am, there may you be also" And where I go you know, and the way you know."
John 14:2-4

I am not completely sure why I was taken to the mountain near the New City, except to allow me to know that it actually exists and that the purpose for doing God's will on earth is a real one. Knowing that the New City does exist gives me an assurance of life everlasting after my physical existence on this earth. I am content just being where it exists.

"BUT AS IT IS WRITTEN: EYES HAVE NOT SEEN, NOR EARS HEARD, NOR HAVE ENTERED INTO THE HEART OF MAN THE THINGS, WHICH GOD HAS PREPARED FOR THOSE WHO LOVE HIM."

I Corinthians 2:9

This situation brings to mind a very familiar visionary who saw God's plan for his life in such a vision. I now fully understand what Dr. Martin Luther King meant by the words in his address to the world in his "**I Have a Dream**" speech. In his speech he speaks of having been to the mountaintop. I believe he too was given an opportunity to see what I have seen, except he was allowed to ascend to the mountain top and see God's New City; prepared for those who will occupy the city when Jesus returns again. I can imagine how much peace and comfort this must have given him during a trouble period in his life.

The book of Revelation also speaks of the New City, and the reference seems to indicate a place God has chosen for us to live after the Second Coming of Jesus. Perhaps one side of the mountain represented physical life; the life I was living at that moment and the other side represented spiritual life (eternal life). I believe that I was not allowed to see the city because I had not experienced, nor was I close enough to my physical death.

"And there came unto me one of the seven angels which had the seven vials full of the seven last plagues, and talked with me, saying come hither, I will shew thee the bride of the Lamb's wife. And he carried me away in the spirit to a great and High Mountain and shewed me the Great City, the Holy Jerusalem descending out of heaven from God."

Revelation 21:9-10

I was not anxious, nor impatient when he said that I would not see the city then, for I knew that eventually I would. Once again my spirit was delighted and at peace. Now it was time to travel again and see more. We once again ascended up.

5-E

THE CHURCH AND THE CROSS

Still in the spirit, the angel and I continued to travel. We were now traveling over the waters of the world. It seemed as if we were passing over a large body of water such as an ocean. What I was experiencing was the feeling of floating in a cloud and moving by thought or spirit. I recall moving across clear skies, and beneath us I saw waters rushing against its tree-lined shores. I could see the foam and hear the water beat against the rocky areas. Then we moved over quiet waters that seemed so vast that there was no end. In all of this I found peace and great comfort.

Now, he that was with me began to instruct me. His thoughts revealed that I should always show a spirit of love and kindness toward people and that there is no real difference in any man, for we are all spirits, from God, the Creator.

Then the Angel's thoughts focused on the church and the people of the world. Once again I was excited and eager to accept the knowledge that was being given me. I also truly appreciated the fact that I was being allowed to experience such a wonderful revelation.

As we moved across the waters he showed me the different churches of the world. He commented to me that it does not matter by what religion people separate themselves, because there is only one **God, The Father: and God, The Son.** All who serve him are equal in his sight. There is only one church. All of those who believe in the **Father, Son, and Holy Spirit** are the Church. People in Christ are the Church and denominations are man-made discriminators and dividers.

Denominations are often based on differing philosophy of how a certain group wishes to worship and serve God or whom they believe

38

is the divine messenger. Many denominational differences are based on ceremony and traditions. So if you are Catholic, Baptist, Mormon, Jewish, Buddhist, Hindu, Muslim or any of the different faiths it means nothing in the end. All of these religious differences will disappear when you come to live where Jesus lives.

There is only one true way to serve God, and that is in *Truth and Spirit*. In the end, God will make no distinction of human faiths, for we will all be as one, because in Christ we are one. (*In other words, what faith you follow or denomination you proclaim is not important when it comes to serving GOD, as long as you serve God in truth and spirit.*)

Further reading in the book of Revelation revealed that the large body of water that we passed over had some relative symbolism.

"And he saith unto me, the waters which thou sawest, where the whore sitteth, are peoples, and multitudes, and nations and tongues."

Revelation 17:15

The waters symbolize the many people that make up and cover the earth, and all of those that make up the different churches of the world. The waters formed one large body, and this is what God's church should be, one large body of believers worshipping and serving God with one purpose, undivided. The first body of water that we passed over, that were rushing and beating against its shoreline and rocks perhaps represented a violent, vicious, turbulent and aggressive people. And the calm waters represented a peaceful, kind, loving and understanding people.

All of the different churches of the world are important and needed, because no one church has all of the answers, nor provides all the truth to its followers. No one faith or religion has all of the truth. Each religious faith adds something different, and together there is a better understanding of the total truth, as well as the true nature of God and his will. As long as any person views his own religion as the only truth, they will never come to a full understanding of the total truth and the reality of God's plan or his nature.

Each religion fulfills a spiritual need that the others may not or can not provide. On earth religions and denominations are how we express the philosophy of our beliefs. As we venture out of our own confined spiritual awareness we gain additional understanding and spiritual growth. At each stage of spiritual growth we begin to think and function at a higher spiritual level. Our knowledge, wisdom and understanding also increase with greater spiritual awareness. There is a Japanese proverb that says, "***When the student is ready, the teacher will come.***"

At each level, as you are ready for the knowledge or insights, God will place it before you, in order that you may continue to grow in understanding and love of him. *God is not interested in religion, but rather our relationship with him, and our spiritual understanding of his love and plan for our lives.* He cares about our spirituality not our religion.

The angel and I were still moving in the spirit, and I was at the height of spiritual and emotional awe. He finalized his thoughts on the Church and people of the world. Then he turned and looked directly at me and said, ***"I have to leave you now."*** Upon hearing those words, a feeling of disappointment, sadness came over me. I was so disappointed that we had to separate.

I was so taken in by what I had been shown and told, that I did not want to return to the world I had left behind. I had prepared my mind for more knowledge and at this moment I wanted to see more and did not want to come back to the physical world.

I just wanted to continue on with him and be in his presence and spiritual knowledge. I recall him breaking the connection between himself and me. When he released me the spiritual connection had been broken. It was as if there was a spark from the tip of his fingers to the tip of mine. There was a small explosion. I began to slowly descend to the earth.

In spite of the feeling of disappointment and sadness of him leaving me, I felt complete. I had such joy, such peace, and my movement was so natural and easy. I did not want this feeling to end. I knew, however that unless I physically died, I had to return to my physical existence.

At the end of our time together the angel left me with a feeling that he knew me and I knew him, beyond just this particular experience. Perhaps we have both been in the presence of God together before. Who really knows? But I thank God for the experience. *Praise God, who is the master of all!*

THE RETURN HOME

As I descended back to the world that I knew, I was wondering where was I going. It seemed as if I was passing through a mist. Initially I could not see anything below me. Then suddenly below me I saw a great multitude of people singing and praising God.

As I came closer I saw that the crowd was standing in front of a large church, facing a large cross. As I continued to descend I could hear their voices increasing. As I came closer it appeared as if they were waiting for something to happen. They all patiently stood there looking to the cross, singing praise to God.

At the end of my descent, I came to rest on the cross that the crowd was standing around. As soon as I touched the cross I felt a surge of life, and energy running through me as if I had been plugged into an energy socket. At that moment, it seemed as if the skies opened up, and there was a great light shining out of heaven onto the cross. It seemed as if light was coming from everywhere, and the singing and the level of the crowd's voices increased.

The cross gave me a feeling of renewed life and announced to my spirit that Jesus' death on the cross is the key to man's salvation and eternal life with the Heavenly Father in the New City. The symbolic sacrifice of Jesus on the cross is the key to life, through his sacrifice our lives are no longer ours but belong to him.

It is not for any one thing that I have done that entitles me to eternal life; but rather what Jesus did on the Cross-that entitles, and grants me eternal life with Jesus and God the Father, in the New City. As soon as I touched the cross, the crowd began to sing and praise God continuously, "A*nd there was an echoing up to heaven.*" And with this praise and singing I transformed back into my physical self.

5-F

REVELATION OF THE
REALITY OF THE VISION

The next thing I knew, I was waking up to a new morning. I was alone because my roommate had already left for class. As I awoke, I could see the clear sunshine coming through my dorm window. This day seemed more energy charged. I was so full of joy and excitement over having experienced something of this magnitude. Nothing had ever touched my spirit, in the way that this journey had. It was something that was never imagined or expected in my lifetime. But the excitement was not over yet.

The experience was so real that I kept asking myself, "Was this a dream? Did I actually leave the room, and perhaps this earth?" Something spoke to my spirit and said it was true and that what I had experienced was not a dream. Upon getting up from my bed, I got on my knees, prayed and praised God for allowing me to receive such a blessing. Then I sat on my bed and began to go over in my mind all of the things that I had experienced. It was hard to contain myself. I did not know what to think or do next.

I got dressed and prepared to go to my regular classes. I kept thinking about what had happen. When my roommate returned I explained to him what had happened, and then proceeded to class.

I just had to tell someone what had happened to me. As in most cases with such experiences, I seemed to be the only one really excited or amazed about the event. I believe that most people believe such experiences are possible, but only get excited, or sincerely believe it when they have similar or unique experiences themselves. I tried telling some of my friends about the vision, but most seemed unmoved by the event, and I felt as if they really did not believe that anything spiritually significant or miraculous had happened.

42

So with all this excitement built up within me, I had to find someone to tell the story of my wonderful and moving experience. I needed someone with a spiritual foundation that would be interested and could share my excitement and enthusiasm. I also wanted to find someone who could help me understand the symbolism and meaning of the things that I had seen and heard.

I constantly prayed for knowledge and wisdom, but I never imagined that God would bless me in the manner He had. I was now searching for the meaning of the vision and things that were shown and told to me.

Each passing day I would find some quiet time and read the Bible hoping for some sign that would reveal to me what I needed to know. I believed that if I were to find the answer it would be in the Bible.

A couple of days passed and I was beginning to wonder if it was just a dream and doubted whether it had some special meaning as I had originally believed. It is amazing how others can sometimes affect your belief in something that you are one hundred percent sure about.

Two days later I was sitting in the student union, reading from my Bible, when a young man approached. He introduced himself and said, "I noticed that you were reading the Bible." He told me that he was involved with Maranatha Ministries and I told him that I was involved with Campus Crusade for Christ. We began to talked about faith and other spiritual matters.

Finally, I had encountered someone whom I felt could certainly appreciate what I had experienced. He appeared open-minded and he appeared to be a spirit-filled young man. This was my opportunity to tell someone what I was feeling and perhaps get some understanding of what it all meant. So I began to share with him my vision and experience.

As I was telling him about the experience he looked at me and began to smile. He said, "*I have a book I want you to read,*" and asked if I had ever read the book entitled, "Vanya" and I said no. I asked what was the book about, and he said that it was based on the true story of a soldier in the Soviet Army named Vanya and the struggles and hardships he endured because he was a Christian.

The following day the young man brought me the book, and I began to read at my leisure. The book mentioned that the young

43

Soviet soldier kept a diary of his experiences and passed them on to his mother who was a Christian woman. The events of the book were so amazing and I was able to see the incredible way in which God had been working in this young soldier's life.

Much of the punishment and brutality he had suffered from Soviet military officials was due to his being a Christian and refusing to deny his beliefs. This was especially interesting to me because I was still a solider in the Army Reserves.

The book spoke of the many miracles that God had worked in Vanya's life, and of Vanya's continued faith. I was quite impressed with his level of faith and all that he endured. I was really moved by the events of this book, not suspecting that the biggest surprise of all was yet to unfold for me in the upcoming chapters.

One day while sitting in my room I read a chapter that caused a surge of emotion to swell within me, and brought tears to my eyes. In the book, after a hard day of training, Vanya laid down to sleep and an Angel appeared before him and the roof of the building was opened up. The angel spoke to him, and said, "I have some things to show you." The angel took him on a journey, and showed him <u>the very same thing</u> that the angel had shown me three days earlier. (*Glory to God*)

Described in the book was an incredible description of the greeting, the quiet place, the same meadow, the same clear stream, the same mountains and the New City. He also had the same fear of snakes that I had, and the angel told him the same as I had been told, "Do *not be afraid for there are no snakes here.*" The angel also told Vanya that he would not see the New City now; just as the angel told me.

According to the book, upon awakening the next morning Vanya's belief was that he had a wonderful dream. But later that morning three friends approached him and asked, *"Where did you go during the night?"* and he said that he had not been anywhere, that he never left the building. His friends said that they had awakened during the night, and out of concern for how he was being treated, came to see him, and found that he was not in his bunk, nor in the building. Upon hearing this, Vanya knew that what he had experienced was real and not just a dream as he had thought.

Amazingly enough, this story confirmed within my spirit that what had happened to me was real. What a confirmation this was. This was so profound. I had to put the book down and walk away from it for a few minutes.

Upon reading Vanya's confirmation I could feel the spirit of the Lord working in my life. I tried to put all of this together. In my mind I summarized the events; first I had the **VISION,** and a day or so later I met someone who gives me a book to read, and after reading the book I discover that a soldier had the exact same VISION and experience that I had, and was given confirmation of its reality. This caused me to be full of emotion and spiritual joy.

At this moment I felt as if in a single moment everything that I had ever wanted to know had been made available to me. For all of this to come together in this very place and time could not have been an accidental occurrence.

Initially I only shared this event with a few individuals that I felt could appreciate the importance of this spiritual experience. I realized that God was sending me a message, informing me that what I experienced was as real as any other experience in my life, and that there was a special message for me to share with others. As stated earlier, I truly believe we exist in an age of spiritual enlightenment.

God truly works in mysterious ways and has a special way of confirming his presence to us. I believe that my serving in the military has something to do with God's divine plan and that one-day it will be made known unto me. Nothing is coincidental in the life of a Christian; there is a reason, time and purpose for everything under the sun.

5-G

GOD PLANTS SEEDS IN US
FOR FUTURE HARVEST

For many years, I did not understand the meaning of the vision. Then, in January 1990—12 years after my vision- while traveling from Fort Leonard Wood, Missouri to Fort Chaffe, Arkansas, to serve as military exercise evaluators, a friend and I, were discussing spiritual matters. He stated that he had gained a lot from reading from the book of Revelation. He insisted that I read the book of Revelation, beginning with chapter 13. Out of curiosity, I followed his advice to see what he felt was so important for me to read.

I began to read and knew immediately that the answers to my questions about the vision were in the verses of the book of Revelation. I knew this was what God wanted me to know and that my vision was not a dream. I was amazed that a book written over 2000 years ago explained the vision I had in 1978.

When I read Revelation 21:5, I knew what God wanted me to do:

"And he that sat upon the throne said behold, I make all things new. And he said unto me, write: for these words are true and faithful."
Revelation 21:5

"And he said unto me, these sayings are faithful and true: and the Lord God of the Holy prophets sent his angel to shew unto his servant the things, which must shortly be done."
Revelation 22:6

Many of the things that John had seen and wrote of in the book of Revelation, were some of the very things that I had seen in my vision, and it was put upon my spirit to write about what was shown to me. I praise God for allowing me to see those things and giving me an understanding of these things and of things to come.

"AND I SAW A NEW HEAVEN AND A NEW EARTH FOR THE FIRST HEAVEN AND THE FIRST EARTH HAD PASSED AWAY. ALSO THERE WAS NO MORE SEA.
THEN I JOHN SAW THE HOLY CITY, NEW JERUSALEM, COMING DOWN OUT OF HEAVEN FROM GOD PREPARED AS A BRIDE ADORNED FOR HER HUSBAND"
Revelation 21:1-2

When you read the above verse you have to ask yourself what is exactly meant by "new heaven" and "new earth." Some believe that this earth will be renewed after the Second Coming. However, if you read the verse carefully it clearly indicates that the old earth and the heavens above it were passed away. The prophet sees a new heaven and earth, not a rebuilt, renewed, reborn, or a recovered earth and heaven.

It can be viewed that God will or has prepared a new planet that is the same as our present earth. Perhaps this is the earth that I walked during my journey beyond the physical.

Scientists have stated that the universe is expanding and new stars, planets, and new galaxies are being born. One has to ask his or herself; why are all these new planets and galaxies being created? Is God speeding up his actions in the known and unknown universe? Does God intend for man to inhabit these new planets? I believe that he does, and that we will live and serve him, throughout the entire universe.

You have to think beyond the normal concepts of new life on this earth. First of all, the earth will be destroyed. Secondly the number of humans who have existed before now and those who will exist before God returns are so great that one or two planets can not support such populations. Our thinking has to change in regard to this idea.

In my heart I say; Glory to GOD for I know he lives and one-day there will be a new earth and a new heaven and I will see the City beyond the mountains. When I pass beyond the physical I will live

47

with Jesus, because of what Jesus did on the cross, giving us eternal life through grace.

6

GOD TAKES CARE OF HIS OWN

After I had an understanding of the various parts of the vision, I began to understand a great deal more about things that happened to me in my life. I reflected back to an incident that occurred while I was stationed in Karlsruhle, West Germany. In October of 1984 I was returning to Karlsruhle, from a construction project that we had been on for 6 months, and I had another near-death experience.

Several days before making my trip, I had taken my car to a mechanic shop in a small German town outside the training area to have my tires rotated and balanced. This was important since I would be doing some high-speed driving on the autobahn.

My car, a Fiat X-1-9, was a small compact sports car and it seemed road-worthy. I had every confidence that it was ready for the trip home.

I got up early that October morning and packed all my books, uniforms and equipment into the small car. I got started on the road, and because it was such a beautiful day, I decided that I would make the drive slow and leisurely.

The drive was relaxing and very scenic: beautiful fall colors were popping out; the air was cool and crisp, but not cold; the sun was out, and its rays were soothing as they passed through the glass of the car. It truly was a beautiful day.

There was very little traffic and I was traveling along the autobahn at approximately 90 miles per hour. Cars frequently passed me at speeds that exceed 130 miles per hour. I decided that I could make better time if I picked up the pace a little bit. I pushed the speed up to 118 miles per hour. At this speed I would make it home in about three hours, as opposed to four.

Suddenly there was a vibration in the front of the car. The entire car started to tremble. Upon feeling the vibrations I immediately took my foot off the accelerator; the vibrations got extremely worse, and the car did not slow down. The steering wheel began to shake uncontrollably and a feeling of helplessness came over me. In one sudden movement, the car was totally out of control, and was being pulled off the road.

The car began to go into a spin. It was spinning so fast that I was pushed back into the car seat, and I could not see nor hear what was happening around me, though I could feel what was happening to the car. At that moment I felt that this would be the end of my life. During that emotional moment, the only words that came to mind were *"God protect me now."*

At a speed of approximately 110 miles per hour the car was thrown into a guardrail on the left side of the highway. The impact was so great that it threw the car back across four lanes and struck the right guardrail. Once again, the car and I were thrown back across the highway to the left guard-rail, which once again threw it back to the right guardrail where it stop spinning and came to a complete stop.

When I open my eyes I expected to see a mangled and bleeding body mixed with steel and paint. I said to myself, "I know that I am hurt now." As I looked down, I saw that my lower torso was intact, and so were my hands and arms. There was no blood in sight. Fearing a head injury, I then pulled down the rear view mirror and was surprised to see that no damage was done to my head or face. I had not received a single scratch. Fearing that the fuel tank could explode, I immediately exited the car. To my surprise I did not receive one scratch from the accident, nor was I nervous or upset. God had heard my cry and answered me.

I was relaxed and truly happy to still be physically alive. I was truly surprised that I survived. Many people have not survived lesser accidents, at much lower speeds. All four wheels of the car were broken and the back portion of the car was completely torn open from sliding around on the highway surface. Items packed in the compact trunk of the car were scattered all over the autobahn. Paper, metal and plastic from the car, and paint from a can of spray paint were also scattered across the autobahn.

If this did not demonstrate the presence of God in my life, and his ability and desire to answer sincere prayers then nothing ever would. Within approximately 12 minutes, the German Poliezi arrived. They asked a few questions and determined that the cause of the accident was due to mechanical failure.

Within ten minutes a wrecker arrived and took me and the car to Ansbach U.S. Military Kaserne, in Ansbach, Germany; approximately ten miles away. When we arrived the driver delivered the car to the installation's morale support impound lot and dropped me by the Military Police station where I filled out an accident report. I sat around in the offices trying to determine the best way to get home. I decided that it would be best to take a train.

The Military Police then drove me to the local train station. I always carried a few German Deutsche Marks on me for emergencies. I went up to the ticket window and purchased a ticket to Karlsruhle. During the ride home, I sat there and replayed the scenes of the accident in my mind. I recall the only words that came to mine during the accident; *"God protect me now,"* and how, that cry had saved my life. Two hours later, I walked safely through the doors of my home to my family: Brenda, Petrice and Charles Jr.

7

MAN IS MORE THAN FLESH

When the Spirit Shines Through

We tend to look on ourselves as physical beings, but we are actually living, walking, and talking spirits. In 1990 I had an experience that made me more aware of this and my own spiritual presence.

In March of that year I attended several non-denominational church services at Grace Covenant Church in Waynesville, Missouri. The minister, named Judith Dodson; was a very wonderful and spirit-filled lady of God. Through participation in the services I learn a great deal more about how to have an effective prayer life, and how to develop close and personal relationship with God.

I believe this church functioned the way a church should, and I saw the true meaning of tithing and fellowship. As I look back now, this was a part of my spiritual growth and maturity.

My spiritual awareness was awakened and I felt the spirit of the Lord move upon me as I listened to the pastor speak and she was truly an anointed spokesperson for God, when near her I could feel the presence of a divine spirit on her.

One night during church services I felt the Holy Spirit upon me. The words of the songs that we were singing and the spirit within the church stirred my emotions and spiritual awareness. It seemed as if I was everywhere in the room at once. I was in spirit and able to see clearly in a 360-degree view, all that was happening. I felt my spirit rise above my physical consciousness. Though this wasn't the first time I had felt the spirit within me rise, the feeling was more intense this night.

After services a young lady named Patricia came up to me and said that she had something strange to tell me. She explained that during the church services, she saw two images: one with a yellowish glow about itself and the other having a whitish glow about itself.

She continued by saying that the image with the whitish glow was standing with the pastor and that the one with the yellowish glow was standing next to me, and that this was not the first time that she had seen this.

I believed what she said. Though I am unsure whether what she saw was the image of *another* spiritual being standing next to us, or if it was the personification of our own spirits showing through, I strongly believed the later; that the images she saw were our own spiritual embodiment shinning through. I feel that perhaps when you are really in the spirit, you start to move beyond your physical body in the true sense of the word.

I have often had the sensation that I was outside of my body looking at myself or seeing everything around me at one glance. It is commonly said, "*We all have an aura.*" An aura is an invisible energy field that surrounds all living organism. It is part of the life force of a living thing that emanates like a vapor of heat rising from a body. Perhaps it could have been our aura's emanating from within us.

No matter the explanation, the connection to our spiritual side was evident by the presence of these spiritual beings, or our own spiritual personification. Once again I had moved in a realm beyond the physical and it felt great. This was a common experience in my life, but this was the first time someone explained what happened during this phenomenon.

This is not something unique to only Pastor Judy Dodson, or myself, but something that all of us as spiritual beings have the ability to do. We all have the ability to reach a state of spiritual awareness and connection with God the Father, where our warm glowing spiritual essence will show through, creating a wonderful light beyond our physical bodies.

In order to experience this condition, an individual must free their mind from everything except the love for God and the desire to serve and do God's will. You must become completely filled with the Holy Spirit in order to rid yourself of all other thoughts.

When filled with the Holy Spirit there is no room for the spirits of hate, lust, envy jealousy, false pride, deceit, or lying; furthermore, there is no room for Satan, for he can not and will not reside in the same vessel with the Holy Spirit. Sincere love for God and Jesus will quickly transform you into this spiritual state.

You have no doubt heard many people speak of having an, "out-of-body experience." Becoming filled with the Holy Spirit is a part of this phenomenon. Most individuals do not know what or why it is occurring, or what to do with the experience. I am sure that others' out of body experiences have been similar to what I have experienced throughout my life. I believe that all spiritual beings can move from their physical state into a more spiritual state if they have enough faith, and awareness of God and the spiritual aspects of life. Focusing on money will move you no where except from one tax bracket to a higher one. And the focus on other physical things will only grant you temporary satisfaction.

Each day my eyes are opened wider and my awareness of the things around me becomes clearer. After many years I am now beginning to understand more about God's plan for my life as he places his desires in my heart. I feel that God is working in my life and will give me all that is needed to accomplish that which He desires of me.

We all must trust in God completely. The more we place our trust in Him, the more we will see the wonders of His works in our lives. We must allow Him to guide us and provide for us.

"Trust in the Lord with all thine heart; and lean not unto thine own understanding."

Proverbs 3:5

All of the event and experiences mentioned up to this point have help me gain a clearer understanding of the vision and what expected of me. Now I clearly understand what moving beyond the physical is about. I understand that I am not just limited to my physical state of mind, nor my physical body. We all have greater abilities that we actually demonstrate. There is a multitude of abilities locked inside our spiritual self. We must learn how to unlock the secrets to our spiritual gifts and abilities by getting rid of all the worldly things that we allow to burden and consume us daily. I know society places a lot of these burdens on us and it is difficult to just shake them off, but we must try.

Moving beyond the physical must become an attitude more than just a mere thought, if you wish for it to happen. By truly seeking a greater understanding of who and what you are many things will be revealed to you. Flesh and bone are only temporary and create a shell for the real you. Remember you are great and wonderful, created in the image of God our Creator. Each of us possesses a part of his spirit. So, imagine if he has great powers, should you not have inherited those powers also?

The following chapters are intended to provide some insights into everyday life. Much of what I speak of has been revealed to me through spiritual messages and experiences. These insights are food for thought and are intended to help open our eyes to possible explanations to questions that have come to mind throughout our lives.

God has given much to many of us, including knowledge, as well as physical and material goods, and we must share them with others in this world.

8

INSIGHTS INTO LIFE AND SPIRITUAL REALITY

Be aware, that no one person or group has all the answers or all the right answers to the questions of life and spiritual reality. Always keep an open mind when dealing with these subjects. Be careful, not to become taken by those that will try to deceive and manipulate you. Most of us are hungry for answers to spiritual questions and there are those who offer us easy fixes to our everyday problems; there are no miracle drinks or magic rags that will cure all you health problems. God the Father and His son Jesus are the solution to all your problems. Remember that God will listen to you and that you do not have to pay anyone to pray for you. It is important to note; God does not charge you for answering your prayers and requests.

We all must be careful not to put too much faith and trust in any man, because they will always disappoint you. You can only put all your complete trust in Jesus and God the Father, and be assured of complete satisfaction. He does not send all men, who claim that God has sent them. Some use the gospel as a way of getting, wealth, power, position or other personal gains. Some do it for sexual gain. However, there are many, God sent men, working in the will of God and willing to do the right thing for their fellow man.

8-A

PURPOSE FOR OUR LIVES

(Why Are We Here?)

Purpose for and within our lives is found in the experiences we gain on earth and in what we learn from sharing with and helping others. Life is a journey of experiences, and eternity with the Savior is the destination. To live with God, and having not experienced all aspects of our present physical human existence might make us unappreciative of God's perfect gifts to us: Love, Peace, Health, Joy, Prosperity, Goodness, Knowledge, and Relationships.

If we never experience *hate,* then it would be difficult for us to appreciate God's world of perfect *love.* If we never experience *war and violence*, then we will not fully appreciate the life of perfect peace and tranquillity, which God has in store for us. If we do not experience *pain and sickness*, then can we fully appreciate God's gift of *perfect health?* If we never experience *sadness, and sorrow*, then how can we appreciate what it means to have *everlasting joy and gladness?* If we never experience *poverty, and suffering*, then what would we have to compare God's abundant gifts and powers that He will give to us? If we never experience illiteracy and ignorance then how can we know what a wonderful thing it is to have *perfect knowledge.* Without the experience of the mortal life of man and physical death, we could not really appreciate the full meaning of eternal life with God.

I suspect that this was the case for Lucifer and the angels that followed him. They had always known the wonderful gifts and power of God and did not have an appreciation for them after billions of years. Not knowing what it was like to not have the blessings of God they became unappreciative. What a sad thought to be locked away forever from the love of God, along with his tremendous gifts.

The purpose of life on earth is to allow us to demonstrate that we are worthy of God's gifts and to help us appreciate all that He has given us as well as what He has prepared for us. God has already given us wonderful things—we just have to obey and live the life he ordered for us: Love thy neighbor as thyself, and Love the Lord thy God with all thine heart and all thine soul. Through this we show ourselves worthy of His Love. He gives unto us all that, which is wonderful, but what will we give of ourselves to others. Will we give a portion of what he has given us?

God created a vast universe, which science has taught us contains millions of galaxies, planets, and stars- much, much larger than just this small planet. I believe that God created this vast area as the home for his most wonderful creation: man. This space was created for us to inhabit, rule, and flourish throughout, so that we can live out God's original plan for mankind.

God's plan, for man was interrupted by sin. Since God cannot stand to have sin in His presence, man was separated from Him. His son, Jesus, took on the sins of the world, allowing man to once again abide with God. When God returns man unto Him, He will resume His plans for man, and mankind will communion with Him forever in a wonderful world.

If we are faithful, over the few things here on earth, God will make us ruler over many in the place set aside for us from the foundation of the world. Perhaps our faith and obedience will earn us rule over a planet somewhere in God's vast creation.

God has promised us gifts and blessings for being obedient and living a righteous life. When Jesus arose from the grave he said; "I have all powers in my hand." The father gave this power to Him after Jesus lived a perfect and righteous life, obeying the Father's will. By this act Jesus showed himself to be the only one worthy of saving man. Jesus demonstrated to the world that a man could live a life on earth without sinning. For his sacrifice Jesus was greatly rewarded.

Before His death, Jesus never spoke of having all powers, but often spoke of the mighty powers of His father in heaven, through which he performed miracles. In performing miracles, He always spoke of performing them in the name of, or through the power of the Father who had sent Him. However after His resurrection He spoke of having all powers in his hand. This appears to be powers given

Him after his long suffering for man's sins. The Father will reward us in the same manner, as long as we are strong and stand against the things that are wrong when confronted by them.

8 -B

Who Is Jesus?

When the name of Jesus is mentioned, many thoughts come to mind. Some individuals consider him to be the greatest miracle of all times while others view him as the most influential element in modern human life. Still there are those who do not believe in his origin, or his claim to be the true living Son of God. Some believe that He existed and was a great prophet. Others believe that he was just a good man who lived during a time when men needed something to believe in.

It is easy and safer to believe in His existence and claim of heavenly heritage. However it is far too risky to not believe in him. If you believe in him and are wrong; nothing loss, but if you do not believe and are wrong, you have tremendous amount at risk.

Who is Jesus and what does He represent to mankind? The most common thought is that Jesus is the Son of God, the Creator of all life and the universe. To truly understand who Jesus actually is, you must first understand the nature of Jesus. God the Father and Jesus the Son are the same in spirit. He who has seen Jesus has seen God the Father. No living man has seen GOD, but to know Jesus is to know the Father; for they are of the same nature, and alike in their spiritual being. The Son is just like the Father, they both are completely filled with love, mercy, forgiving kindness, truth, life, and peace. There is no difference in their personalities, character, or desires. They are two separate spiritual beings but are identical in every respect. The Holy Spirit is also similar to the Father and Son; this is why they are said to be one because they are in one accord. When we love we show the spirit of God that is within us. The true nature of God and Jesus is complete Love.

We are made in the image of God and the other heavenly hosts. It is written that, in the beginning, God announced that man would be made in his own image:

"And God said let us make man in our image, after our likeness"
Genesis 1:26

"So God created man in his own image in the image of God created he him: male and female created he them."
Genesis 1:27

Jesus represents the one by whom mankind is saved and reunited with God the Father. Jesus links man to God. Man's sinful nature had severed the bond between himself and God, because God can not be in the presence of sin. Because of Jesus' sacrifice God has given him authority over man.

Who is better suited than Jesus. He lived the life of a man, and experienced all the conditions that mankind has to endure. He knows of the difficulties of being human. He understands when individuals struggle with the many issues of living a sin-free life. So he is well suited to speak for mankind in the presence of God the Father. That is why it is so important that we pray to Jesus, and ask him for our blessings.

The Father still hears our prayers and answers them. We must recognize Jesus, for what he sacrificed, to become flesh and save us from eternal death because of sin, thus bringing us back into fellowship and communion with God the Father.

References For Jesus

Jesus represents different things to many people. Who would you say that Jesus is? Jesus can be described and identified in numerous ways:

Son of God most high; God the Son; Lamb of God; God's beloved son, in whom He is well pleased; Son of man; the Christ; Savior; Lord and Savior; Mercy and Salvation; God with us; Master; Lord; Prophet; Teacher; Healer; Messiah; Peace Maker; Sweet Rose of Sharon; the Light; our Elder Brother; the Lilly of the Valley; the Bright and Morning Star; our Strength; the Good Shepherd; the Miracle Worker; the Living Bread which came down from heaven; Bread to the hungry; a Rock in a weary land; Shelter in the time of storm; the Church; the Foundation of the church; the Temple of God; the Resurrection; Mary's son; the Light of the world; the Truth and the Life; the Way; the Lord of all; the Author and Finisher of our faith; the Resurrection and the Life; Life Eternal; the Word; our Refuge; our Salvation; King of the Jews; King of Kings; the First of those born again; He is Love; the One by whose name man is saved; He who sits at the right hand of the father; He who was God and became flesh; Wisdom from God; is Faithful; He who stands at the door knocking; He who will baptize you with the Holy Ghost and fire; He who came not to call the righteous, but sinners to repentance; the Living Water from which you drink and shall never thirst again; the Name by which repentance and remission of sin should be preached; the True Vine; He that is in the Father and the Father in Him; He who has all powers in his hand; the Great Deliverer; He who overcame and conquered the world; *He is Knowledge, Wisdom, Power and Love*, but most of all he is "the Christ, Son of the living God.

When we say that Jesus is the Light, it brings to mind something that I have heard often. When most individuals experience near-death situations, they often speak of "walking into the light." They describe this light as one that penetrates all, and draw them towards it. Jesus is the light at the end of the path. He draws the spirit of man to the next stage where peace and complete life are found. Since he has been given charge of mankind it is natural for him to be in this position. For he will deliver us to the Father.

When we walk toward the light, We are walking toward Jesus and to the Father. In the light is love, truth, knowledge, and understanding; the very things Jesus came to earth to bring us. The everlasting light shines on all, to show us the way to live and the way to salvation.

The statement that Jesus is Salvation is very important to our present day life and eternal life. Jesus came to earth to show us the way to salvation. He is the one true and only way of salvation. A person has to believe that he did come to save man, that He did die, and He did rise again and still lives today. Jesus is Life.

The life that is in us is a part of God's own spirit, broken off and placed into our physical bodies along with our souls. Jesus is Life, and through Him we have complete and everlasting life.

When Jesus was on the cross, he was saving all righteous mankind from eternal death. His death saved those that had died before Him, those that were alive, and those yet to be born. After his death on the cross, He went on to free those that had died before His coming. What a wonderful act of love, and a tremendous gift to man.

The list of phrases, and words listed earlier help to express how man view the identity of Jesus Christ. I believe that He is: The Light, Our Salvation, Truth and the Life, the First of those to die in the flesh and ascend up to Heaven, the One who was truly perfect in the flesh, the Example for our lives, and our Elder Brother in spirit.

Perhaps the best way to sum up who Jesus is can be gained from this statement: Jesus is the one true living son of God, who came to earth to save man kind, and in the process, died for man's sins and now sits at the right hand of the Father, and by whom man can be saved to once again have a relationship with God the Father. He is my personal Lord and Savior.

C

Judging Others

One of the things that humans do often is to sit in judgment of others. Despite the fact that we lack true knowledge by which to judge others, we insist on doing so. Only he who possesses perfect knowledge can know exactly what is right versus what is wrong, and can rightly judge anything or anyone. Only God has perfect knowledge and knows what man's true purpose is and what he truly should be; therefore, only He can judge that which He has created. We do not know God's plans, yet we often try to do his job. God the Father is the true judge.

Instead of judging with your eyes, learn to observe and listen with the spirit. The eyes and ears can only observe that which is physical. In the physical world it is difficult to understand truth and reality beyond what we hear and see. Through our spirit we can understand much more.

The spirit can penetrate beyond the surface of things and into the innermost depths. Using our physical senses it is difficult to discern what is truth and what is reality. The spirit can find truth and reality because the spirit is a part of that truth and reality. The spirit and truth are perfect and everlasting. The flesh is imperfect and temporary.

God tells us to "*judge not, for yet by the same shall ye also be judged.*" If we judge, then we shall be judged, by the same imperfect standard by which we judge others. We must forgive others not judge them. We must become love finders and not fault finders. We often find fault after a single glance, but nearly always fail to find the good or special qualities.

We have been doing this for so long that it is difficult for us to not judge when we look on another person. I feel fairly safe in saying that when we judge, seventy percent of the time we are wrong. This is one of those areas of our lives that we must work at.

We insist on others meeting our standard of living, thinking and acting. Who or what is to say that what we think, feel, believe or know is right?

Allow others to be happy with whom they are. If a person desires not to be rich, that is OK. Do not come down on the individual because wealth has little importance to them. There are greater things to be valued in life than wealth and riches.

We must accept all people for who they are and what they are in life. We do not have the right to be intolerant of anyone because of their race, color, religion, status in life, or economic condition. God is very tolerant of us in our state of need. We can very easily end up in the same predicament as the poor and needy. This thought should keep us humble enough that we never look down on anyone. God has put something of greater value within the heart of those who love.

8-D

=====================================

What Really Matters

=====================================

We all have our own beliefs about what matters. But in the true sense of life and humanity, what really matters?

<u>Love</u> is the one thing that really matters in this world. True Love is the absence of hate, evil and unrighteousness. God is Love and His love is the force that connects everything in his creation. We are all linked by His spirit, which penetrates everything. The essence of God is love.

We must always remember that life and love are eternal; that life is entwined around love; and that without love, there is no life. <u>Of all the things we do in this world, only love and what we do for others, last</u>. They are the only things that can transcend beyond the physical. We must express the love of God, which is in us, by being constantly mindful of the needs of the poor, homeless, sick and disadvantaged.

There are Angels that walk among us. Their purpose is to remind us of the need to help others and to help us in our daily lives. Angels sometime will take the form of a poor or disadvantaged person in need. By doing so, they stimulate our spirit of giving and helping.

The only thing we can take with us from this life is "the good that we have done for others, and the love we shared. All else fades away and is the vanity of man, for all that we build up on earth other than goodness, love, kindness and righteousness is done in vain. As soon as we pass beyond the physical it has no meaning at all; it is the same as the dust or the wind. Our greatest joy and riches will be found in our charity, and our love.

This brings to mind another incident in my life. One Saturday I was shopping in a small mini mall, just outside of Fort Leonard Wood. I passed an old gentleman who stopped me and asked me for a dollar. I quickly sized up the situation and came to the conclusion that he was trying to hustle me. So I simply replied in a manner that most people do, "I don't have it." I knew that this was not true. I am sure that I had at least ten dollars in cash on me at the time. But I quickly judge the man and denied him the blessing of a dollar, which I surely could afford.

Just as soon as I had said those words I began to regret having said them. There seemed to be something different about this man, I could not figure out what it was. I took a few more steps and turned to my wife and said, "I am going to go back and give the man what he wanted." I must have walked no more fifteen seconds from where I saw the gentleman, but when I turned he was not there. I said to myself, "I know that he didn't just vanish."

I spent close to five minutes looking in the crowd and in the shops near where I saw him, but he was not to be found. So I put the money back in my wallet and caught up with my wife.

When I denied the man of the dollar, it struck me as strange that he made no expression, nor indicated any dissatisfaction with my refusal. I thought to myself, "The man I just turned down was perhaps an angel, testing my spirit of giving, and I refused to give him a small portion of what God had so graciously given me. The man could have been Jesus himself, exposing my true spirit of giving and judging.

That particular situation bothered me for the next seven days. I had always believed in giving to the needy, but instead of just giving, I made a quick judgment about the man and denied him a small blessing.

From this incident I came away with the philosophy that it is not up to me to judge, just give and let God do the judging. If someone request a blessing from others under false pretense, God will deal with them, all we have to do is give with the desire to help others. There is no way to tell how much of a blessing that I missed out on by my poor judgment decision.

The joy of giving and sharing is wonderful. When you give God gives back to you in even greater amounts. We must not be selfish about the possessions that we are allowed to use during our lives on earth. All the things we "own" are items temporarily loaned to us by God during our earthly stay. That stay is an extremely short one.

Compare the seventy and up to one hundred years a man can lives on earth, with the trillion and trillion of years we will live during eternity. That is why the things we do on earth are not worth our eternal soul. *Why enjoy a fleeting moment of pleasure and miss out on an eternity of joy and wonder?*

It is sad that racial prejudice, religious intolerance, ethnic bias, and hate can enter our hearts and cause us to lose out on a tremendous gift. So I say to you, pray unceasingly that God help us to look past any differences, and love all as they are. God himself will punish those in violation of his laws, so be not overly concerned with getting back, or even with others. God can do a better and longer lasting job than we can.

Religious faiths, denominations, ethnic backgrounds, race, nor financial position really matters in the true light of life. *These things only have the value that we assign to them.* When God looks at one of us, he looks far beyond those insignificant details. What matters to God is the spirit and soul of the being.

The two most destructive forces on this earth are fear and hate. These two forces along can destroy a civilization, a world, a universe and even an entire life form. On the other hand the two most powerful forces on earth are love and kindness. These forces can make the strongest man weak and the weakest man strong, respectively.

Another one of the things that really matter is this world is <u>people</u>. Caring for and about people really does matter. People have become so consumed with their own worries that they feel they do not have the time to be concerned about the trouble of others. This is where we fall short. If we do not show compassion and empathy for others we will soon become so disconnected that we will loose that compassion so critical to maintaining a peaceful world. Once our compassion is gone, it will facilitate the unmerciful treatment of all humanity. This was what was starting to occur with Adolph Hitler and the Nazi party in Europe in the 1940's. Member of this party had no reservations at all about committing all manner of cruelty against the Jewish population of Europe. Their cruel and brutal actions resulted in the death of over three million innocent people. When there is no compassion it is easy to treat another human like a stray dog or unwanted animal.

We must show the love that God intended for us to show toward each other. We must strive to help those who are less fortunate in this life. That is where real joy and purpose is found.

8-E

<hr>

The Continuous Effects of
What We Say and Do

<hr>

Have you ever throw a rock or an object into a pond or body of water? Of course, most of us have. When observed you notice that each object sends out ripples when it strikes the water. Notice how the ripples start small and in the center, then get larger and spread out over the entire pond or body of water. Most things we do in life have the same effect.

Everything we do in life has a ripple effect. If we spread hate and discord, it goes out and affects others, who in turn treat others they encounter in the same manner. Eventually it spreads far beyond us, but returns again to us through others, who may have a nasty attitude or just refuse to work well with others on certain issues. If we spread love, it ripples out and causes others to feel good and treat others with kindness and they in turn do the same to others they encounter, which returns to you and affects you in a positive way.

If you do good deeds as a man or woman, then goodness will find you and follow you throughout your life. The same goes for evil and bad. Nothing leaves this earth-the bad that is created floats around on the earth, searching for someone to overcome. Therefore what you send forth will return to you eventually. It is important that we say and do positive things.

To demonstrate the effect of how things spread quickly, I remember a situation dealing with some strawberry plants from my garden. One Saturday morning I was in my garden transplanting strawberry plants. Two years earlier I had set out about forty strawberry plants. During this time the area where I had planted the strawberries stayed dry and grew weeds. I had not tended the plants during that time, and I feared that most of the strawberries were dead. When I went to dig up what remained in the garden to transplant, I found that not only had many of the plants survived, but three times as many plants had grown from them. I observed that each surviving strawberry plant had thrown out runners and was producing at least one or two new strawberry plants.

Good and evil grow in the same manner. Whatever we plant; whether it is goodness and righteousness, or wrong and evil, it will throw out runners and create the same sentiment somewhere else in the world. When you go to view what has become of what you planted, you will find that it has spread far beyond where you originally planted it.

Words themselves have a great deal of power. They have greater power than most people give them credit for having. What you say has the ability to cause things to materialize. Words can harm or help. Words can build or bring down; they can create or destroy and they can heal or curse.

Strong faith in what you say causes those things to come to pass. It is the same faith that Jesus spoke of in His life. If you say to yourself that you are sick, guess what; you will begin to feel sick. If you tell yourself after a long run, that you are not tired, you will not feel the effect of being tired. This is the attitude that soldiers in training use to overcome difficult moments. Your body will believe whatever you tell it, especially if you believe what you are saying.

That is why parents are warned; that telling a child that he or she is dumb, stupid or slow will often cause the child to take on those qualities. The opposite is also true: if you tell a young lady that she is beautiful and intelligent, soon she will begin to appear more attractive and behave in a more educated manner. That is why real beauty and ugliness are not physical features, but rather mental and emotional attitudes. We must guard our tongues and control our actions. Our words may cause harm or damage when we do not wish to do so.

A case in point is my performance during the first two years of high school. I was busy on the farm and did not put the amount of effort into my studies. I made Cs and Ds, and was somewhat satisfied with the grade. During my eleventh grade year, one of my teachers said to me, "Charles you have a great deal of potential, and I know that you can do better in you studies than what you are doing." She asked me questions about my study habits and my home life, and made recommendations to me on how to study. She said, "I want you to try this for a while and let me know how well you are doing afterwards." Those positive words changed my whole world. During the remainder of my eleventh grade and twelfth grade years I made A's and B's.

We all deserve a chance to do the best we can in life. Negative words and negative thinking will prevent that from happening.

8-F

Expectancy Yields Much

At some point in your life, you have probably heard the phrase, "You get what you expect." This is true: if you expect good things to happen, then good things will happen; if you expect bad things to happen, then bad things will happen. This is the basis of positive thinking, which is the root of faith. Often time you receive because of a strong belief and an expectation for something to occur. It is possible that we possess the power to will things to happen.

Expectancy is so very important in our lives, because expectancy brings about fulfillment. That which we expect will be brought about by our faith and the power of the human will. There is tremendous power in a strong conviction about a particular subject or idea. Expect it to be there, believe that it will be there and what ever it is that you believe in will be there for you. You can bring that desire into reality through your own faith, will and conviction.

Fulfillment of our desires is based on faith in things hoped for. We should hope for and expect all great things.

In His caring, loving and graceful way God always provide for us. We must remember this even when we do not know what we should expect. We must expect Him to give us the very best.

8-G

Focus Of Life

You may wonder, what should be the focus in this life, in order to make the best of our time on earth. One part of the answer to this question is, "*Focus on the spirit not the body.*" Make the body a slave to the spirit, and not the reverse. We all must be mindful that the body is not and should not be the main focus of life.

The spirit and soul are the main elements of life and the essence of our being. The body is a temporary vessel, but the soul and spirit are eternal and everlasting. Man may be able to destroy the body, but only God can permanently destroy the spirit and soul of a being.

However, we must attend to the physical needs of the body as well. Neglecting one element of this two piece combination will leave you unfulfilled as a person. We must show great respect for the body since it is the temple, which houses our spirit and soul. The spirit and soul are the treasures of life itself.

Being healthy and conservative about what you do to the body is very important. We must be careful about the activities in which we engage our bodies. The simple habit of body piercing is harmful if not done properly or if done to certain parts of the body. Most individuals who have the multiple piercing in their ears do not realize that every major organ in the body has a nerve that runs into the ear. Pierce the ear in the wrong place and damage to one of the major organs can occur.

Good physical conditioning of the body and mind is a critical element for living a happy life. This conditioning helps the body to withstand great amounts of pain, stress, and pressure. However the spirit remains the primary component and the essence of life.

Caring for the body, yet neglecting the key needs of the spirit is a terrible thing to do to one's self. Spiritual awareness, enhancement, growth and maturity are much more important than the same physical attributes. Never focus on feeding the body at the risk of starving the spirit. It is better to be physically hungry than spiritually hungry. Luke 12:4,23 says:

"And I say unto you my friends, be not afraid of them that kill the body and after that have no more that they can do." 23. "The life is more than meat, and the body is more than raiment."

These important verses teach us that the body is not the most important part of life, yet we focus so much on its pleasures. Today we feed our bodies to excess, but are our spirits so fat and full?

Many people pay large dollar amounts to wear name brand clothing. These items have no real value other than that which people place on them. Some people care more about being dressed in these designer items than about the health and life of the poor and unfortunate. While it is all right to have and enjoy wealth and material things, do not allow them to become the focus of life.

Physical death is momentary and a temporary state, but spiritual death is permanent and is the real death, which occurs in the heavens and earth. Therefore we must strive to move beyond centering on the needs of physical body.

Learning to Focus

When individuals learn to focus, they begin to understand a lot more about everything. When I was in my late teens and early twenties, I discovered a unique God-given ability to focus on the behavior of people—their mannerisms and actions-and was able to predict what they were going to do next, as well as what they would say next to whomever they encountered.

This ability was developed in my early years when I was filled with amazement at the wonder of God's creation, and how it all interacted. I was quite amazed by the abilities of the human mind.

While growing up on the farm, I would intently observe everything around me: birds, butterflies, cattle, dogs, insects, etc., watching how they acted and reacted to the environment around them. I was very curious about what made creatures do what they do.

On any given Sunday, you would find me watching the television adventure show, "Wild Kingdom," which provided me a great deal of knowledge that I was unable to obtain from direct observations. I soon began to understand the nature of most things around me.

At this point in my life, I was not involved in many social or extracurricular activities. Most of my time was spent working on my father's farm, and my mind was not occupied with much more than simple everyday matters. I did not have the worries and concerns that many others had to deal with, and therefore, my mind was able to focus clearly on all aspects of the activities around me. One of the most educational experiences of my life happened when I would visit and talk to older citizens in our neighborhood. From them I gained a great deal of knowledge about people, life and life's situations.

As I got older, I bean to socialize more with people away from the farm community. I began to apply my focus and observation skills to the behavior of people. I watched how they interacted and related to others and the world around them. It was amazing to see that most people followed definite patterns, very similar to the animals and creatures I had observed.

The perception was unbelievable, and as I mentioned before, my ability to predict what individuals would to do next increased substantially. I was even able to predict with a great deal of accuracy the next words an individual was going to say. I knew this was a gift from the Lord. One down side to this was, I was starting to develop a bad habit of completing people's sentences for them. I quickly realized that this could be quite annoying, and stopped completing sentences verbally.

I continued to practice this throughout my college years. It became somewhat of a hobby.

Upon graduating from college I entered the military and the everyday world focused on getting ahead. As time passed, my focus changed direction—I became focused on getting ahead, dealing with, financial issues, early marriage problems, working with difficult people, and all of the other problems that people deal with in their daily lives. Before long, I had lost that sharp edge of perception and no longer focused on the actions of others, but rather on how to survive myself.

Problems and cares of the world take away from our ability to focus on what is really important: God and the spiritual aspects of life. Focusing on physical aspects of life will only grant you temporary satisfaction. However focusing on the spiritual growth will yield eternal gratification.

8-H

———————————

Death is Rebirth

———————————

One comfort that believers in Christ can find, is the knowledge of having everlasting life. For those who are in Christ you will never die.

But they, which shall be accounted worthy to obtain that world and the resurrection from the dead, neither marry nor are given in marriage: 36. Neither can they die any more: for they are equal unto the angels: and are the children of God; being the children of the resurrection.

Luke 20: 35-36, 35

Many have believed for years, that death was a sort of sleep or holding pattern for the spirit, and that it is a realm where spirits abide while awaiting the Rapture. After His death on the cross Jesus descended down into Hell and locked the gates and then ascended up into paradise where he unlocked the gates of paradise to release all those who had died before him. Those who were in paradise were allowed to go on into heaven, for Jesus had paid the price for their sins.

Because Jesus paid for our sins, there is no death of the spirit, and upon your physical death, your spirit moves from the body in a natural transition. The transition is automatic because the spirit can no longer use the body. The spirit is totally aware of everything happening at the moment of physical death. It is drawn to Jesus for He is our Savior. Those that are in Christ are naturally drawn toward Jesus, the light of the world, the Truth and the Life.

Jesus is that light that draws spirits unto Him. It is the light that people experiencing near death report that they see and are drawn toward. Those who are not of Christ are tied to the things of the world, and resist the light; because they know not the nature of God, and are afraid of what the light holds for them. All that are in Christ automatically go into the presence of Jesus. There is no waiting for the Rapture before you see Jesus.

One example of the spirit instantly being with Christ is in the clear message that was given on the cross, when the thieves were speaking to Jesus. Luke 23:42-43 says:

"And he said unto Jesus, Lord, remember me when thou cometh into thy kingdom. 43. And Jesus said unto him, verily I say unto thee, today shall thou be with me in paradise."

Jesus said that the very day the thief would be in paradise with Him, not sleeping until He comes again, not in limbo, but present with Him. You are an eternal being, and if you are in Christ, you will never see death as a spiritual being. Your physical body may die or cease functioning, but your spirit will live forever.

Jesus cautioned us in his teachings not to fear death. He stated in Luke 12:4,23:

"And I say unto you my friends, be not afraid of them that kill the body and after that have no more that they can do." 23. "The life is more than meat, and the body is more than raiment."

We fear death because we have not personally experienced anything other than the life we presently live here on earth. But Jesus knew that the life we live here is only a preparation for a much greater, fuller and more rewarding life, beyond this world.

Death is a reality, and we all have to deal with it at some point in our lives. We have to deal with the death of a parent, husband, wife, brother, sister or someone very close to us. We have to go through a period where we adjust to that person not being there for us to interact with as we did before their death. We often feel sad and lonely because we are left behind without the comfort of their presence.

Before my mother's death in June of 1998, I saw the spirit of death coming closer to her in the last few months of her life, and told myself that when it happens I would be ready for it. I felt prepared for the death, but I was not ready for the emptiness her absence left in my life and in my heart. This is the difficult part for humans to deal with.

The feeling of emptiness is understandable because we all help to make up the life force of the world and each other. We are all interconnected as spirits, because we are all part of the one total spirit, and that is the spirit of life, which comes from God. All of our spirits come from his enormous and wonderful spirit.

Six months after my mother's death, my father died. I knew then how to deal with the emptiness that death leaves and was better able to cope with it. I knew that my parents were not gone forever, only gone from here. That offered some comfort. After the emptiness and loneliness pass you begin to focus on the continuation of life, knowing that they still live on somewhere. I know that today they are continuing to live out their lives in the way God had intended for man to always live- in harmony with Him.

Death is not an end but a new beginning for life in a realm beyond the physical world. We must prepare ourselves for the journey and live in a manner satisfactory to He who created us, and He will judge whether or not we are worthy to live within His presence and love, for eternity.

We must live our lives so that we please God. God will not have unrighteousness, sin, or evil in his presence. Sin is simply disobedience of God's word and will. In the end, death and destruction will be the result of our disobedience and it will not be limited to just man. In II Peter, 2:4 it reads:

"For God spared not the angels that sinned, but cast them into chains of darkness, to be reserved unto judgment."

If God will not spare the angels, then we must realize our susceptibility to God's Judgment. The choice between life and death is ours. So choose life.

8-I

The Effects of Trying to Control Others

Life is a wonderful gift, and should be experienced to the fullest. We all have the freedom to enjoy all of its wonders. One thing that will help us enjoy a much fuller life is, if we allow others to also live their lives to the fullest.

We should be mindful that we do not own anyone, not even ourselves, and therefore, we should not attempt to control others in a negative sense. We are to kindly offer advice when we see a person in need or headed in the wrong direction, but this does not give us the right to attempt to control others. In the next three sections, the topics of controlling others, children, and spouses are addressed. At some point in our lives we will all have to deal with some of the issues addressed in these topics.

How We Should View Others:

We should see others as spiritual beings needing our help and being worthy of our love and time. We must learn to look past the physical and see the inner most part of a person. Some call it the heart of the person, but in reality it is the spirit of the individual. The spirit is the true person, not of all the physical decorations that make up the body. The human body is a wonderful creation and a miracle itself. We should appreciate the beauty of the body but we must learn to look beyond the physical to see true beauty, which is the beauty that resides in a loving, giving, sincere, kind, and forgiving spirit.

I feel sorry for those who go through this life focusing on race, color and differences. Race isn't everything and everything isn't about race. All who focus on this aspect need to wake up and start understanding what's really important in this life.

God made men different for a reason. It is not for one to think that they are better than the other is, but a more divine purpose. Understanding what is really important, is a big problem for many individuals; they tend to focus on what's important in this <u>world.</u> All of that which is in the <u>world</u> is temporary and fades away.

Won't the racists and bigots of all colors be surprised when they leave this life, and they see with whom they will spend eternity? Only then will many of them truly understand that it makes no difference? And we will all live together for eternity. God is not going to put up with any prejudice or hatred. Man might as well start learning now how to love one another and how to look beyond the physical. We are all brothers and sisters in Christ.

We deal with many people in our daily lives. We have brothers, sisters, husband, wives, neighbors, and friends that we interact with on a regular basis. Life is much more enjoyable and fuller when we allow others to be who they are.

How We Should View Our Children:

To have children in our lives is truly a blessing. Children are free and individual spirits just as parents and adults are. It is the parents' responsibility to teach and develop their children in the way they should grow.

As parents we do not own our children. They are not ours, for they belong to God. We are only caretakers; vessel through which their bodies are brought into the world. All other aspects of their being belong to God. God is the real father and mother of mankind.

We share our lives and our experiences with children and they share theirs with us. God made every living thing, and all things belong to him. No man owns another; we are all on loan to each other.

Children are young spirits who need to be cared for and taught the benefits of the experiences that we have already been a part of. In the true sense of time, we also are young spiritual beings. We teach our young, and in return they teach us certain things. One of the greatest things that they teach us is unconditional love.

One key responsibility that we have in raising our children is to teach them to be responsible and respect all things. This comes through discipline. When I say discipline, I am not only talking about the discipline they receive when they do wrong, but the discipline of their mind, spirit and body.

It is important that we make corrections when they do wrong. This may sometime take the form of some style of physical discipline. There are times when we will need to use disciplinary actions to get their attention or encourage children to do what is right. This is part of the human condition, where we respond to things that make us uncomfortable or cause temporary pain. We need to continuously encourage them in the reading of Holy Scriptures, to help them strengthen their spiritual knowledge and awareness.

We need to encourage them in the area of critical thinking. They must be able to think for themselves. They must be able to reason things out. Skills such as reading, writing and understanding higher level math, help to develop better thinking skills.

The time we spend with our children allows us an opportunity to help them learn the lessons of life, and help them to avoid some of the problems of the flesh. Their mission is to learn from us, apply the lessons to their lives, and pass on the lessons to those they bring into the world. We should be teaching children about God, Love, Forgiveness, Spiritual Awareness, how to gain understanding, and how to deal with the world around us. They, like us are here to learn about the world; not become consumed by it.

How We Should View Our Spouses:

God commanded: *"Husband love your wife, and wife love your husband."* Husbands and wives are partners in marriage. Neither one owns nor controls the other. They both share in the raising of the children, with neither having more say than the other on the raising of a child. Most of all, they must respect each other and allow each other to be individuals in the context of being a married couple.

"Being as one," means working as one toward common goals within the marriage, not giving up your individuality. This requires the sharing of ideas and dreams. In order to function as one, we must have love and trust. Our spouse should be our friend as well as our lover and mate.

One of the key elements in a good marriage relationship is agreement on who will be the leader in the home. There is a difference between leader and boss. A leader lovingly directs guides, and makes the path clear, whereas a boss is the one you work for. Every organization has to have a good leader in order for it to be successful and move ahead, and this includes a home and family.

It would be nice if everyone could be the leader, but that does not work. In a situation where there is more than one leader, confusion is always present. The leader has to be fair, responsible, truthful, tactful, moral, decisive, reliable, responsive to the needs of the others in the family, and courageous. The individual that fits that description deserves to be the family leader.

Many marriages suffer due to communication problems. There is never room for abuse in a marriage. It is said that God hates divorce. This does not mean that a man or woman has to stay in an abusive and otherwise dangerous situation. It is also true that he hates cruelty, physical abuse and brutality. God gives us common sense; he placed the sense of fear within us to be a warning sign for danger in order for us to move out of harm's way.

It is difficult for one moment to believe that God wants a woman or man to stay in a situation where their continued presence will end in death. Even though God will deal with abusive husbands or wives, it is hard to believe that He wants a partner to stay there and take the constant beatings and abuse that some married women and men suffer.

It is important for young people to understand the necessity for knowing as much as possible about the person that they intend to marry, before the go through with the ceremony. Normally, people do not change after the marriage. Many times, individuals marry and hope that they can change the partner once they get married. The result of this is disappointment for the person hoping to change the other. When they discover that they can not cause a change, they develop anger and bitterness for the other partner.

That is why it is so important for young people to take time and experience being their own person before marriage. Individuals should have some time for themselves. They need to experience having their own individual freedom, personal bank account, automobile, and place to live. There is nothing greater than having the freedom to come and go as you please.

To never experience these personal freedoms will cause frustrations in young people who marry without first being able to experience them. After experiencing these aspects of individuality, then they will know who they truly are.

Prospective couples should seek some type of marriage counseling prior to getting married. This will allow some question to be raised that they will not know to address prior to marriage. Most things can be worked through during the marriage, but there are some that must be dealt with prior to making the commitment.

8-J

Understanding God's Purpose
And Desire for Man

One of the apostles once asked Jesus, "W*hat is man that God is mindful of him*." When you look at the nature of man, and then look at the nature of God, this is a question that would naturally come to mind. God created the heavens and the earth and placed all the living things upon it. Then He created man in His own image and placed man over all that He had created. God created man in his image for two reasons: first, when God looked down on the earth He wanted to have a presence and see Himself walking amidst His new creation. By creating man in His image, he made it so. Second, He wanted to be able to have fellowship with man; therefore he gave man his image. If man looks like God, it is easier for God to relate to this new being.

As humans we all desire to associate with those who look similar to us and have similar characteristics and ways. This is why people of similar racial groups associate more with each other than they do with others of different racial groups. God's desire was for man to have the same nature as Himself. We have the nature of God in each of us. But sin has placed a rift between God and man. We must strive continuously to have a close and personal relationship with God. When I say personal, I mean having the same type of relationship with God that you have with your mother, father, wife, husband, boyfriend, and girlfriend.

We must talk to God daily, ask Him questions, tell Him our troubles and carry on a two-way conversation with him. When you start to see God and Jesus in a close, personal relationship, then you will begin to see them as close family and beings with which you can associate, and not just some mystical and unexplainable beings or spirits.

Our God is an approachable God. You can talk to Him as often as you need to, and go to Him with any problem. It is His desire that we communicate with Him as we journey through life. God is large enough to be everywhere in the entire universe and yet compact enough for you to take everywhere you go. He is everyone's God and he is your personal God.

When man fell from the grace of God, the Creator did not give up him. God knew that he had created something wonderful and good. If you created something that was wonderful and it served a good purpose, you would not destroy it because it had a few flaws. No, you would repair it and make the changes necessary to make it function correctly. That is exactly what God has done for us. Man was broken and needed fixing, so God sent the only repair person, who had enough knowledge about the subject and who was qualified to do the work correctly. That repairperson, sent by the Father, was Jesus. Jesus came and fixed everything that was broken with man. He installed a new power source and operating program, and then started us in the right direction. We are so blessed that Jesus was available and so highly qualified.

The nomadic Australian Aborigines have one of the clearest views of living and personal relationships with each other and the Creator. They thank God, or the "Divine Oness," continuously and are faithful that He will provide them with all that they need, and yes, they get it on a daily basis.

For many years, so called civilized man has pushed his religion on the native inhabitants of each continent around the world. In some cases this was well needed. But in some, it may not have been needed. For if individual already believe in a divine creator and live with their fellow man and nature in the loving manner in which God intended, then they have already achieved what God wants.

If you look at the beliefs of all the native inhabitants of all the continents, you will find a close similarity in their beliefs about God, or the Supreme Being. All the native tribes of the various continents have a respect for nature and God, that is lacking in so-called civilized man.

God allowed His son Jesus to appear, some 2,000 years ago, to a people who had forgotten how to love, share, communicate, and engage in fellowship with each other and Him. It was necessary for His son Jesus to come and teach and demonstrate to all, how to love, live and treat each other, as well as how to show obedience and love to **GOD** the Father. For those living in accordance with God's will there is no need to send a savior. Only those who are in violation of His will require saving from themselves.

The Australian Aborigines, Native American Indians, North American Eskimos, South American Incas and other native people of the world, had perhaps already arrived at a stage of life where they had a clear understanding of the creator's desire for their existence with Himself, nature, and their fellow man. We see in movies, books and other stories that the American Indian was not very tolerant with the telling of lies and deceiving others, but with the arrival of the early settlers, many undesirable things came into their world.

The Native Americans respected nature and everything in it, because they knew God, (whether or not they used that particular reference). Perhaps they did not refer to Him in the same manner as we do, but they knew of His existence. They gave back to the land and took no more than they needed in order to live. They shared with all and possessed nothing that belonged to the earth. Most native people had the same philosophy. They believed in living as one with nature.

Today, we have taken possession of all the land that was once open for all to use and enjoy. We trap and cage animals and take away their freedom. We have also managed to cause numerous species of animal to become extinct or near extinction since our arrival on the shores of the Americas. Such actions are in contradiction to the philosophy of living in harmony with God and nature. Man must refrain from destroying everything that he comes in contact with.

Most of the native populations possessed a spiritual awareness that we today are searching for. We have a hunger that is not satisfied by the riches and physical possessions of the world. We have, and can do more today, but we are not content and happy with this world of abundance, because it is not fulfilling and satisfying. Only God can give us this, because **GOD** is Love. Love is the element that connects everything in the universe. It is the "Universal Force" that causes many unexplained things to occur around us in our day- to-day lives. When I speak of Love, I am not referring to that feeling a girl and a boy experience when they have an emotional attachment to each other. This Love is a much greater power, or phenomena.

Even our own spirit possesses more power and ability than we know how to utilize. The spirit and soul are the only things about us that are permanent and eternal. To understand the nature of the spirit will take you beyond this world.

Physical death was brought into this world by lies and deceit, but truth is what can take us beyond physical death. First we must be truthful in all we do. We must search for truth, for its insights will free us from the bonds of the flesh, and allow us to understand more in this life. We have all heard the old saying, "You shall know the truth and the truth shall set you free." We will become free from the worries and pains of this world. This is the freedom we should desire.

We are spirits first and physical beings second. More accurately, we are spiritual beings within a physical body. We are part of a whole: God is the whole and we represent pieces of His loving spirit, broken off and placed into physical bodies with a soul. The day will come when we will have another body, but it will not be made of flesh and bone. It will not be made of anything which can die, rot, break down, tear, leak, nor in any manner less than what it starts out to be.

It is clearly a mystery what we will do when we arrive where Christ is, but I am assured that it will be wonderful. There is no mention of man's destiny other than worshipping God the Father, continuously. I feel assured that there are wonderful missions for us to fulfill. If we are faithful over the few things that He gives us charge over on earth, then perhaps we may be given charge over one of the billions of planets in his vast and wonderful universe. Surely He has not created all of this to be a vast celestial wasteland of dead planets and stars, void of life. Surely you can look into the sky on a star-filled night and understand this. It is too much and too great to just be for no reason. And that is just what we can see with our physical eyes. What we do not see is billions and billions times greater than what we see. Yes, it is mind boggling when you think about it, but one day it will all be clear.

Man is God's special creation. It is possible that this special creation is off limits to all other living beings that existed before God created man, except for the angels. Perhaps we are special and kept separated from the rest of His creation, until we are ready to live out the purpose for which He created us.

One possible purpose for man is to assist God in His rule over the universe. We are created in His likeness and may serve as His ambassadors' through-outs the universe. Because we are in his likeness, those we encounter will know that we are from the Creator. What a beautiful and wonderful thought that is. Therefore we must prepare and make ourselves worthy of that privilege and responsibility.

When you ask yourself what we will do in heaven, do you believe that we will "just walk around heaven all day"? I doubt it very seriously, that we will spend trillions and trillions of years, in one place walking around singing and praising. We will sing praises and take His greetings and love to the entire universe. Perhaps we will continue to evolve into a much higher level of spiritual being, in the same way that we move from our physical form to our spiritual form when we complete our earthly tasks and die. With trillions and trillions of years to learn and develop skills and abilities, I don't see us not advancing in some way to a much higher awareness and level of existence. I believe our move into the spiritual realm will be the real beginning of our growth as spiritual beings.

Jesus has already told us of our true nature. Jesus has made it known that we shall be like the angels. In Luke 20: 34-36, He states:

"34. And Jesus answering said unto them, The children of this world marry and are given unto marriage: 35. But they, which shall be accounted worthy to obtain that world, and the resurrection from the dead, neither marry nor are given in marriage: 36. <u>Neither can they die any more: for they are equal unto the angels:</u> and are the children of God; being the children of the resurrection.

When it comes to imagining what is in store for us after this life, I often think about the phrase used in the parable about two servants given charge of talents by their master. In this parable one servant invested and multiplied his master's talents and was told:

"Well done good and faithful servant; you were faithful over a few things, I will make you ruler over many things."
Matthew 25:21

This is a message for us to consider. If we are faithful over the few things God gives us here on earth, great will be our reward in heaven.

So often I have heard ministers and fellow worshipers say they are living to see the Pearly Gates, and Walk the Streets of Gold. But I say to you, I am living to be where Jesus is. Whether the gates are made of iron, brass or stone does not matter. It does not matter to me if the streets are paved with gold, granite, grass, glass or rocks; just to be in the Holy City will be its own reward. Thank you Jesus for giving us this future.

We must live each day in a manner that shows our worthiness of God's love and gifts, and be ever considerate of each other. We are God's servants; doers for God. We are to do for others, what He would do. Let us go forward in our lives and live out God's true purpose for us, here on earth as well as what He wishes of us in heaven. Let us go forth and love all mankind; not that you have to love what they do, but love the people. And judge not, but let God judge, for He can do a much better job, and has a punishment for doers of wrong and evil. None of us have a Hell or Heaven, to which we can send anyone.

I give thanks to GOD and JESUS for everything that I am, and all that I will ever be. For all that I am is because of Him. And with each passing day I long to once again experience the revelation of God's plan for our lives and see more of what He has planned for us. Praise the name of God forever.

"Life is a journey, and the journey never ends."

ABOUT THE AUTHOR

I, Charles Gaskin, grew up on a small county farm in rural Vicksburg, Mississippi. Growing up in the rural south during the fifties and sixties was difficult, but rewarding. Life was somewhat simpler then and people were more centered on truth, spirituality, and the common good of all. During this time, families were closer, and as a matter of fact, whole communities were more like large families, and not just a bunch of people thrown together by chance and economic conditions.

In those early years most Americans were living in rural areas, and many of them on small farms. This was prior to the great migration to the inner city. We were living at what most people called the "poverty level." We did not know that we were poor, because almost everyone around us was in the same condition. Physically and financially we may have been in a state of poverty, but spiritually we were not impoverished. In the midst of poverty we were still able to find happiness and joy.

The early fifties and sixties seemed to be a wonderful time, with wonderful people. Growing up with six brothers and four sisters did not allow much time to be alone. We kept each other company and provided a great support network for each other. As stated before, my brothers and sisters were more than just family they were also my best friends. During my life I have always felt the presence of someone special with me, even those times when I seemed to be alone.

Living on the farm during my youth was a key factor in shaping my life and helping create my appreciation for all life and everything that God has put here on earth for us. Most of my spiritual development and growth took place on that farm. Upon completing high school I attended Utica Junior College where I received an A.S. Degree in Drafting and Design Technology. After completing junior college, I join the Army Reserves. This was a most enlightening and fulfilling experience, because it was here that I truly began to understand who I really was and experience the power of faith.

After being in the Reserves and working for a few years I returned to school at Mississippi State University, where I earned a Bachelors degree in Landscape Contracting and Architecture. I also earned my commission as a 2nd Lieutenant in the United States Army through the Army ROTC program. Fifteen years later I received a Masters degree in Management and a Masters in Human Resource Development from Webster University at St. Louis, Missouri. It was while on active duty that most of the meaning and understanding of my experience and vision was revealed to me.

While on active duty I had a variety of assignments in Europe and the United States, and each one has added greatly to the experiences in my life. Today I teach at a local high school in Jackson, Mississippi, in hopes that I can make a difference in the lives of inner city and at-risk youth. I have a small farm and raise fruits and vegetables with hopes to expand in this area. I would like to one day establish a training program, which will teach young men and women basic Agricultural and horticultural concepts which can lead them to starting their own businesses.